JOE: ONE MOMENT AT A TIME

JOE
A MOMENT
AT A TIME

BRAIN

SENSORY

MAGGIE

ADAM HARDAKER

MR ADAM HARDAKER

Dedication

For my family - especially Michelle, George, Oliver, Charlie, and Henry the heart behind every word I write.

And for all the children we fail to understand, and the families we fail to truly see.

You deserve better.
You deserve to be heard.
You deserve to be met in your world - not just ours.

Author's Note

This book matters because people matter.

Especially the ones whose worlds are built a little differently - not broken, not wrong - just different.

Joe is one story. One child. One voice.

But really, it's about all the children we often misunderstand, overlook, or try to fit into boxes that were never made for them.

This story is my way of saying:

Let's stop trying to bring kids into our world... and start meeting them in theirs.

Let's see the person, not the label.

Let's learn their language, their rhythms, their needs - even when it takes time.

Especially when it takes time.

Because when you truly see someone - not just their behaviours or their routines, but their heart - you start to realise how much they've been doing to meet us halfway all along.

If this book helps even one person pause, ask a better question, or make one child feel a little more understood - then it's done its job.

Thanks for stepping into Joe's world.

Adam Hardaker

How to Use This Book

This book is a journey - one moment at a time.

There's no right or wrong way to read it, but here are some gentle suggestions:

Read together and pause often.

Talk about how Joe feels - and how Maggie learns.

Let the "Between Us" pages guide discussion.

Use the questions to open up conversations with your child or students.

Don't worry if things don't always "click" - the point is to try.

This story is a window for some, and a mirror for others. Either way, it works best when we slow down and truly listen.

Resources and Support (UK)

If you'd like to explore more about autism and neurodivergence:

National Autistic Society - www.autism.org.uk

AmbitiousAbout Autism - www.ambitiousaboutautism.org.uk

Autistic Girls Network - www.autisticgirlsnetwork.org

Contact - www.contact.org.uk

IPSEA (SEND Legal Advice) - www.ipsea.org.uk

This story doesn't explain everything, and it's not meant to. But it can be a doorway to empathy, understanding, and support.

Disclaimer

This is a work of fiction.

Joe is not based on a real child, and Maggie is not based on a real guardian.

While many of the routines, behaviours, and experiences described may resonate with families and children, every neurodivergent person is unique.

Autism is not one story. This is just Joe's.

The aim of this book is to build understanding, encourage empathy, and help readers of all kinds feel a little more seen - or a little more open.

For rights or permissions, contact: ahardaker@hotmail.co.uk

Facebook - Adam Hardaker - Author

Instagram - Adam_Hardaker_Author

THE NARRATOR'S TALE

Before the Story Begins

This is a story about a boy who lost everything, and a woman who didn't expect to be chosen.

The boy's name is Joe. He is eight years, nine months, and twenty-three days old.

He likes toast with no brown bits, numbers that end in even digits, and the smell of buses more than cars. He does not like surprises. He does not like when people speak in hints. He does not understand why people ask questions when they already know the answers.

Joe is autistic. But more importantly - Joe is Joe. The woman is Maggie. She is sixty-four years old.

She used to dye her hair but doesn't bother now. She never expected to raise a child again, especially not her grandson. But here she is, with cupboards full of the wrong cereal and hands that fumble when they try to do things right.

She is not Joe's mum. She knows this. Joe knows this. It sits between them - like a radio left on in the next room. Joe lived with his mum and dad until last winter.

There was a car crash. He remembers parts. A song playing. A cold seatbelt. Lights that came too fast.

Now he lives with Maggie. This story begins not at the moment of loss, but at the moment just after when people try to carry on. When mornings still come, even though everything is different. When breakfast must be made. And shoes must be found. And no one quite knows what to say.

This is not a story of fixing.
It is a story of noticing.
Of missteps, patience, and the quiet spaces in between.
You'll hear from Joe.
You'll hear from Maggie.
And sometimes - you'll hear from me.
Let's begin.

CHAPTER 1: THE NEW HOUSE

Narrator's Take

Developmental Note: Transition & Trust Formation Begins

◆ ◆ ◆

Joe's Part - *Too Much, Too Soon*

I counted the bricks on the path again.
Seventeen.
Always seventeen.
The same as before.
That part was okay.
But everything else was wrong.

The taxi smelled like onion crisps - the sharp, greasy kind that stick in your throat. The backseat was sticky under my legs, like old jelly. The buckle of the seatbelt pressed into my hip, cold and square. My rucksack strap had twisted twice and cut into my shoulder. I could've untwisted it if I'd taken the whole thing off. But then people would look. So, I didn't.
Maggie was waiting on the doorstep. She waved like she was at a parade. Her jumper was purple. Not blue. Mum wore blue when she said things would be okay. Blue meant safe. Purple didn't mean anything.
I didn't wave back.
When I stepped inside, three smells hit me at once:

- A candle pretending to be cookies. Too sweet. Too fake.

- A dog I couldn't see. Damp, woolly, hidden.

- Change. Real change. It smells metallic, like coins pressed to your tongue, like zips pulled too fast.

Change makes my stomach bubble in the wrong way.

Maggie said, "Welcome home, Joe."

But this wasn't home.

My toothpaste wasn't in the bathroom. Instead, there was a swirly blue-and-white one, bright and fizzy. Mine is plain. Plain is better for mouths. No fizz, no burn.

The kettle made a noise like it was angry. It clicked before it hissed. At Mum and Dad's house, the kettle just hissed. One sound. One job. This one had too many steps.

She made toast.

The wrong bread.

Too thick.

Too bumpy.

Too... toast.

I chewed anyway. Like cardboard. My jaw clicked every time, echoing up into my ear.

There was no seat chart at the table. I don't sit unless I know the place has been earned. Dad used to say "gold star for guts" when I managed new things. I hadn't earned this table yet.

So, I stood.

Maggie asked if I wanted jam.

I didn't answer.

She said, "It's okay if you're a bit quiet today."

But I wasn't quiet. I was loud in my head. The words were all piled behind my teeth, hammering to get out, but the lock was stuck.

She showed me the bedroom.

New sheets. Too stiff, like paper before you crumple it.

New pillow. It smelled of fabric softener, not mine.

A soft toy I didn't know, staring with shiny eyes.

No Goodison Park poster. No players frozen mid-run. Just blank walls.

She said, "I put your clothes away in the drawers, nice and neat."

That made my arms go tight.

You don't touch someone else's drawers. You wait for the system.

My hands flapped even though I told them not to. They beat the air, fast, sharp, like birds stuck inside.

I sat on the floor by the door. Always the door. Facing the exit. I tapped the floor four times, then breathed in fours.

In. Two, three, four.

Out. Two, three, four.

The carpet smelled faintly of polish, too shiny, too strong.

She sat too. Not close - that would've been pressure. Not far - that would've meant leaving. Just in between. Waiting.

Then she said the right thing.

"I don't know the rules yet. But I'd like to learn."

I didn't nod.

But my hands stopped flapping.

Which is like a nod.

For me.

❖ ❖ ❖

Maggie's Part - *Boxes of Grief*

He didn't smile. Not once.

I'd ironed his favourite jumper - the soft blue one with the badge stitched crooked. The one from the match his dad took him to. I thought seeing it folded neat would tether him.

I even tracked down the same cereal bowl online. Paid more for postage than for the bowl itself. It arrived yesterday and I'd unwrapped it like treasure. I thought it would matter.

But he didn't look at it. Not once.

He stood in the hallway, clutching his rucksack like it held secrets. Knuckles white, lips tight. His eyes fixed on the light switch as though it had betrayed him.

I said, "Welcome home," but the words rang false. Too bright. Too staged.

He didn't say anything.

The toast was my mistake. Thick-cut seeded loaf, wholesome, fibre-filled, "good for growing boys." I thought I was being clever, prepared. He chewed like he was taking a test. His jaw clicked with every bite.

He wouldn't sit. Just hovered, circling the table like it was lava.

I offered jam.

Nothing. Not even a flicker.

Then the kettle clicked before hissing and he jolted. I'd never noticed kettles had patterns before. Of course they do. Of course it matters.

So many things I don't know.

I thought the bedroom might be safe ground. Fresh sheets, his old duvet cover, a cuddly lion scrubbed clean. But he looked at the drawers like they were traps. Then he dropped to the floor, back against the door, eyes locked on the handle as if ready to bolt.

I nearly cried then. Not because he was unkind. He wasn't. Not at all. But because I felt like a guest in my own home.

So, I sat too. Not close, not far.

And I said the only thing that felt honest.

"I don't know the rules yet. But I'd like to learn."

He didn't nod.

But his hands stopped.

That felt like a start.

Maggie's Notes

- Purple jumper = wrong. Blue = safe.

- My handwriting loops = unsafe. His block letters = safe.

- Wrong bread = wrong day.

- Kettles have patterns. Don't ignore them.

- Flapping = signal, not defiance.

- Don't fill silence. Let him lead.

- "I'd like to learn" = bridge.

◆ ◆ ◆

Between Us

Joe's World

Joe enters a house where everything is slightly wrong: smells, textures, sounds, even kettle clicks. For him, these aren't background details. They're alarms. His silence isn't emptiness. It's noise he can't let out. His flapping, his tapping, his breathing rituals - they're his language of survival.

Maggie's World

Maggie tries hard - ironing jumpers, ordering bowls, baking bread. But her effort isn't the same as accuracy in Joe's world. She learns that love isn't enough unless it listens. By admitting she doesn't know the rules, she earns a fragile sliver of trust.

The Narrators Take

Some stories don't begin with a bang. They begin in silence.
A door closes. A suitcase is set down. A light flickers on in a hallway that smells nothing like home.
This is the kind of chapter that doesn't announce itself. It just... arrives. Like change often does. Uninvited, uncertain, and soaked in someone else's routines.
For Joe, this isn't just a new house. It's a test.
Can the walls hold his rules? Can the fridge hum the right tone? Can this woman - not Mum, not a stranger, but something in between - learn the shape of his world without flattening it?
For Maggie, this is a hallway full of doubt. She's not here to replace. Just to remain. To be the one who doesn't walk away. But that kind

of presence comes heavy with pressure.

So begins their orbit - not close, not far, just circling. Two people trying to measure each other's gravity without causing collapse. Not a new beginning. But a necessary one.

CHAPTER 2: THE FIRST BREAKFAST

The Narrators Take

Developmental Note: Foundations of Co-Regulation and Non-Verbal Communication

◆ ◆ ◆

Joe's Take - *Wrong Box, Wet Spoon*

The clock said 7:01.

I'd already been awake since 6:13. I knew because I'd counted. Every blink of the TV's standby light. Every creak in the ceiling. Seventy-two blinks. Twelve creaks.

Seven o'clock means breakfast. One minute past is late.

Mum used to say, "The day doesn't start until the spoon hits the bowl." That was the rule.

Maggie didn't say anything. She was still in her dressing gown, belt trailing along the floor like a tail. It whispered on the tiles. Not how mornings are supposed to sound.

She made cereal. Same brand, wrong box. The safe one has an orange stripe. This one had a red stripe. Red means stop. Red means wrong. Red means emergency. I don't eat red-box cereal.

I didn't sit.

I walked around the table. Four loops. Tapped each chair leg twice. Then stood by the back door, staring at the sky. Medium-grey sky. Not bright, not loud. Medium is safe enough.

Maggie said, "I've made your favourite."

But she hadn't. She'd made her idea of my favourite. That's different.

I opened the fridge. Yoghurt wasn't in the front. Hidden behind the butter. Hidden means gone.

I pulled out a spoon. Wet. That's not allowed. Wet spreads taste from other foods. Wet means wrong.

My hands went hot. My chest fizzed. My arms flapped. Not to fly. To push out the too-much.

Maggie watched. She didn't say stop. That was good.

She crouched a little, pen still in her hair from yesterday, and said, "What did I miss, Joe?"

So, I pointed. The cereal box. The spoon. The fridge.

I didn't shout. That's progress.

She said, "Right. Let's try again."

This time we did.

I sat. Just for three bites.

But that's three more than yesterday.

❖ ❖ ❖

Maggie's Take - *Guesswork & Quiet Wins*

He was already up when I came down. Cross-legged on the floor, tracing a line between skirting board and tiles with his finger like a surveyor marking boundaries.

I thought I'd done well. Remembered the brand. Thought that was the battle won.

It wasn't.

He wouldn't touch it. Just circled the table, rigid as a soldier on drill. His eyes flicked between the red stripe and the back door like he was deciding which enemy was worse.

I tried. "Your favourite," I said, my voice too light.

He didn't answer. Didn't sit.

He opened the fridge. Closed it. Opened it again. Like a lighthouse beam circling for the same ship.

Then his hands. Fast, sharp flapping. Not tantrum. Signal. His way of saying, *Help.*

I remembered what his mum had told me: *It's not bad behaviour. It's a warning, like steam from a kettle.*

So, I asked, "What did I miss, Joe?"

He didn't speak, but he pointed. Box. Spoon. Yoghurt.

He was telling me. His language.

So, I said, "Let's try again."

This time I dried the spoon. Put the yoghurt front and centre. Swapped the red box for the orange.

And he sat.

Three bites. That's all.

But for him - and for me - it was a win.

◆ ◆ ◆

Maggie's Notes

- Red stripe = danger. Always orange box.

- Wet spoon = contaminated. Always dry.

- Yoghurt must be visible. Hidden = gone.

- Flapping = signal, not misbehaviour.

- Don't assume. Ask. Let him show.

- Three bites = progress. Celebrate small wins.

◆ ◆ ◆

Between Us

Joe's World

Routine isn't habit. It's protection. Every detail - box colour, spoon dryness, yoghurt placement - is part of his shield. One break and the shield cracks. His flapping, pointing, and tapping aren't stubbornness. They're communication.

Maggie's World

Maggie learns the hard way that effort isn't enough if it misses detail. But she also learns the power of asking instead of correcting. By letting Joe lead her through the mistake, she turned a meltdown into three bites - a mountain climbed in his world.

Narrator's Take

Some lessons are learned before a word is ever spoken.

A wrong cereal box. A damp spoon. A yoghurt hidden behind butter. These aren't small things - they are breaches in the blueprint. To the untrained eye, they're quirks. To Joe, they're the pillars of control.

This is where safety lives: in repetition, in placement, in rules that stay put when everything else shifts.

Maggie doesn't know the rules yet. But she does something more important - she asks. She doesn't fight the signs or fill the silence with guesswork. She watches. She listens. And when he points, she sees.

Communication, in its truest form, isn't always about speech. Sometimes, it's a glance toward a cupboard. A quiet refusal. A set of hot, flapping hands that scream: not this way, not today.

Maggie's learning that love isn't shown in the things she thinks he needs. It's in noticing what he's trying to say without words. It's in changing the spoon.

And for Joe, it's progress. He doesn't shout. He doesn't run. He points.

That's how trust begins. With a cereal box. With a second try.

With someone who's willing to get it wrong - and then try again.

CHAPTER 3: THE BUS RIDE

The Narrators Take
Developmental Note: Sensory Thresholds, Flight Responses & Environmental Overload

◆ ◆ ◆

Joe's Take - *Stops, and Starts, and Stops Again*

I knew it would smell like wet metal and other people. Buses always do. The floor, the seats, even the air tastes like coins.

Buses are not quiet. They growl when they move, hiss when they stop, grumble when they turn corners. But I know their noises now. Like monsters with patterns. Predictable monsters are safe.

We walked to the stop. I counted six drain covers. The fourth one was cracked. I didn't step on it. Cracks mean falling. Cracks mean danger.

The sky was medium grey. Not boiling. Not loud. Medium is okay.

Maggie asked if I wanted to press the button for the bus. I shook my head. Buttons are sticky. Sticky means trapped.

The bus was late. My chest tightened like a belt pulled too hard. My breath did the fast thing.

In. In. In.

No out.

So, I bounced on the spot, heels knocking the pavement, to keep from spilling over.

When it came, we sat in the third row, left side, window seat. The safe seat. Not too close to the front, not too close to the back. Right in the middle where the balance lives.

Someone had left a crisp on it. Greasy, bent. I brushed it off with my sleeve, never my hand.

I opened my matchday book. I write in it when I ride buses. Badge man. Chip shop. Stadium gates with their iron teeth. The drawings keep the order safe.

Two stops in, a baby started crying. Sharp, sudden, piercing. I covered my ears, pressed my palms hard. My hum started without asking - my space cartoon theme, low and steady, buzzing in my throat.

I leaned into Maggie's arm. Not for hugs. Just for shield.

She said, "Nearly there, Joe."

She always says that at the bend in the road where the big tree flashes past.

The baby didn't stop. But the words reminded me: the pattern was still intact.

That helped.

◆ ◆ ◆

Maggie's Take - *Learning the Loops*

He didn't speak on the way to the stop, but his lips moved. Silent numbers, eyes fixed on the pavement. He was counting. Steps, cracks, drain covers. Something invisible to me, but vital to him.

When the bus was late, he rocked back and forth. Small, contained. His way of holding the tide. I wanted to say, "It'll be here any second," but I bit it back. Words can spark, not soothe.

We got the right seat. Third row, left side, window. I didn't even ask this time. I've learned. His safe seat has become my habit too.

He brushed off the crisp with his sleeve, neat and precise.

Then out came his little book. Pages filled with gates, scarves, maps. His shield. His world in lines and boxes.

Then the baby cried.

His whole body stiffened. He pressed himself into my arm, clamped his hands over his ears. Not for closeness. For protection.

I didn't say, "It's okay." Because it wasn't.
I said, "Nearly there, Joe."
Same point on the route. Same phrase. Same anchor.
And his shoulders dropped - not fully, but enough.
Enough to carry on.

◆ ◆ ◆

Maggie's Notes

- Counted drain covers. Cracks = danger. Avoid.

- Third row, left side, window = safe seat. Always.

- Buttons = sticky. Don't push him to touch.

- Matchday book = shield. Respect it.

- Baby crying = overload. Anchor phrase = "Nearly there."

◆ ◆ ◆

Between Us

Joe's World
Buses are storms of sound, smell, and surprise. To survive, Joe builds shields - counting covers, brushing crisps with sleeves, sketching maps and gates. The seat he chooses isn't preference. It's survival. His humming, his hands over ears, his leaning against Maggie - these are his language of overload.

Maggie's World
Maggie learns that reassurance doesn't mean "fixing." It means anchoring. She doesn't tell him the baby's cry is nothing. She doesn't push him to press the button. She echoes the pattern instead - the phrase at the bend in the road, always the same. And that makes her part of his map.

Narrator's Take

Buses are built for movement - but they don't move softly.

They jolt, hiss, beep. They carry the chaos of other people's mornings: phones ringing, engines coughing, shoes squeaking on rubber floors. Voices boom and change pitch without warning. The windows show a blur of motion while the inside stands still.

For Joe, this isn't travel - it's tension. The moment he steps aboard, his nervous system is already trying to make sense of the noise, the light, the nearness of strangers.

Behaviours emerge.

He doesn't make eye contact. He tugs at his sleeve. His fingers twitch in small, repeated circles on his knee. He leans ever so slightly away from the man talking too loud behind him. When the brakes screech or someone laughs too suddenly, Joe flinches like a fuse has blown behind his eyes.

These aren't behaviours to correct. They're data - his way of signalling that he's reaching the edge of comfort, the point before panic.

Maggie watches, uncertain. She doesn't always know what each signal means, but she sees enough. She plants her feet beside his, holds out a mint like a peace offering, lets him sit by the window.

She's not rescuing him. She's holding the rope while he steadies himself.

There's no meltdown today. No retreat into silence or sudden bolt for the door. Just signs. Subtle shifts. A boy scanning the storm for an anchor.

It isn't a calm journey. But it's one they finish together.

And that, in itself, is progress.

CHAPTER 4: THE SHOPPING LIST

The Narrators Take
Developmental Note: Executive Functioning, Transition Management
& Meaning in Repetition

◆ ◆ ◆

Joe's Take - *Noise, Lights, Crowds*

I don't like the supermarket.
It's full of wrong noises. Not sharp ones - sticky ones. Echoes that bounce from shelf to shelf. Hums from the ceiling lights. Shoes slapping tiles. Trolleys banging. Fake music leaking from speakers. Too cheerful. Too fake.
I hold the list in my hand. My list. My handwriting. Maggie's loops are unsafe. Mine are blocky. Walls I can stand behind.
The list says:

- Milk (red top).
- Cheese (mild only).
- Chicken slices (not round).
- Green grapes (long box).
- Custard creams (yellow packet).

If one thing isn't there, we leave without it. No swaps. Swaps are lies in disguise.
The air stinks of floor cleaner and raw fish. Someone's perfume cuts through - lemon mixed with fire. It stings.

A man brushes past. His coat sleeve touches my arm. Static shock. My hand curls into a claw. That keeps it safe.

Maggie doesn't talk. That's good. Talking in here feels like shouting.

Then the tannoy buzzes. A voice bursts out of the ceiling - loud, sudden, thick.

Then a beep from the checkout. Another. Then the freezer fans start their drone.

Too many at once. My brain doesn't stack them. It drops them. They smash.

I tug Maggie's sleeve. My claw hand stays curled, tucked tight. Signal.

She sees. She says, "To the quiet aisle, yeah?"

I nod. Three times. Fast.

We walk. Slowly. My trainers squeak. My breath does the fast thing.

In. In. In.

Out. Out.

The quiet aisle has a sign: *Sensory Friendly Hour.* Lights dim. Music gone. The buzz stripped away. Not silent. But better.

I tick grapes. Custard creams. Yellow packet.

I carry them myself. Rule: if I carry it, I scan it.

I place them on the belt. Square. Neat. Lined up.

The trip is nearly safe.

◆ ◆ ◆

Maggie's Take - *One Packet at a Time*

He hates supermarkets. I see it before we even walk in - his shoulders high, jaw tight, hand gripping the list like a lifeline.

The list is his handwriting now. Blocky, straight, sharp. Mine loops too much. I get it now. His letters make him safe.

We start okay. He checks the milk, the cheese, the grapes. Each tick on his list is a stone in a wall.

Then the tannoy crackles. A man's voice booms out. I see Joe stiffen. His hand curls into that claw shape I've come to know - the signal.

I used to think meltdowns had to be loud. Now I know they can be silent. Too silent. His stillness is louder than shouting.

So, I don't tell him it's fine. I don't say, "Nearly done." I just watch his hand. And when he tugs my sleeve, I ask, "To the quiet aisle, yeah?"

He nods. Quick, sharp. His answer.

We walk there. Slowly. I match his pace, even when others huff and push past.

The quiet aisle is dimmer. Softer. The sign says *Sensory Friendly Hour* - lights low, music off, fans reduced. It's not perfect, but it's enough for him to breathe again.

He finds his biscuits. Custard creams. The exact right yellow.

I don't put them on the belt. He does. Neat, careful, precise.

One packet of biscuits. To anyone else, nothing.

To us, everything.

◆ ◆ ◆

Maggie's Notes

- His handwriting = anchor. Always use his list.

- Brushing past = static shock. Keep space.

- Tannoy, checkout beeps, freezer fans = overload. Watch for the claw hand.

- Quiet aisle = reset button.

- He carries → he scans. Rule, not request.

◆ ◆ ◆

Between Us

Joe's World

Supermarkets are storms. Sounds, smells, touches all crash together. His list isn't fussiness. It's armour. The claw hand, the tapping, the breathless nods - all language. The quiet aisle isn't luxury. It's survival space.

Maggie's World

Maggie once thought shopping was about speed - in, out, done. Now it's about patience, shields, and choices. She doesn't fight the list. She follows it. She doesn't rush him. She matches him. That's how one packet of biscuits becomes a victory.

Narrator's Take

Shops have rules. Not the written kind - but sensory ones.
The lights are too white. The fridges hum in different tones. Music floats above the shelves, interrupted by beeps at tills and trolley wheels that wobble on uneven tiles.
For Joe, the shop is not a place of browsing. It's a mission. A list. A route. An expectation.
Deviation creates distress.
Today's plan was clear in his head. He rehearsed it all morning: We go in. We get the things. We don't talk to strangers. We don't look at the sweet stand. We don't go the wrong way.
But Maggie forgets. Or she improvises. She swaps items. She chooses a different aisle. She asks if he wants to pick the fruit.
That's not on the list.
Joe's response isn't loud. It's immediate, physical. His feet stop moving. His jaw clenches. His voice comes out as a flat "No." He breathes faster. His hands squeeze into each other. Not a tantrum. Not rudeness. A rupture in the map.
There's an attempt to regain control - pacing three steps forward, returning to the original spot, scanning the shelf for something that should be there but isn't.
Maggie clocks it. She says, "Back to the start, yeah?" and they return to the entrance. It's not about being difficult. It's about re-

JOE: ONE MOMENT AT A TIME

setting the system.

When they complete the list in the original order, Joe exhales through his nose. Not relief - but release. A signal that the wires aren't as tangled anymore.

He may not say, "That helped."

But his body does.

And Maggie learns, again, that sometimes the best way forward... is briefly stepping back.

CHAPTER 5: THE NEW SCHOOL SHOES

The Narrators Take
*Developmental Note: Sensory Processing, Anticipatory Anxiety & Loss
of Familiar Anchors*

◆ ◆ ◆

Joe's Take - It Hurts Where No One Sees

The shoes were stiff.
Too new.
Too shiny.
Too not-mine.
My old shoes had soft backs where the leather bent. They slid
on without me untying the laces. That's how shoes should be -
knowing my feet, bending with me.
Maggie held up the new ones. Black, polished, smug. They shone
under the light like they wanted to blind me.
She said, "We've had these since before Easter, Joe. Time for new
ones."
She didn't mean to ruin things. But she did.
The new shoes smelled wrong. Plastic and cardboard and glue.
Not my smell. Not the smell of playground grass or warm rubber
or my socks.
I tried one. Just one.
It pinched. Hard at the sides, rough on the tongue. Touched places
shoes shouldn't touch - ankle bone, soft toes.

I pulled it off fast.

Maggie tried again. "It's just different. You'll get used to it."

No. Different is danger.

I folded my arms. Bricks across my chest. Looked at the clock. Ten minutes late for my Saturday checklist. Tick-tock beating too loud. Wrong shoes. Wrong time. Wrong everything.

My hands twitched, then went to my old shoes.

Maggie watched. She looked tired. Shoulders dropped, eyes lined.

Then she did something good.

She got the old shoes.

She let me hold them.

I sniffed them. My smell. My dirt. The scuffed leather bent to my shape. The sole pressed with my pattern.

Then she took the old laces, the frayed but safe ones, and swapped them into the new shoes.

She put a soft sticker inside too - the kind that feels like cotton, not glue. Stickers mean calm. Cotton means safe.

Then she said, "We can try again tomorrow. No rush."

I looked at her. Then at the new shoes.

I touched them with one finger. Not to wear. Just to feel.

Still wrong. But less wrong.

Maybe tomorrow.

Maybe.

◆ ◆ ◆

Maggie's Take - *The Shoe That Changed it all*

They were just shoes. Brand new, right size, breathable lining, memory foam. Everything the man in the shop said would be perfect.

Except they weren't. Not for Joe.

He hated them on sight. The look, the feel, the smell. His whole body braced like he was about to be attacked.

I nearly said the thing adults always say - *You'll get used to them.* But I bit it back. Those words never helped me when I was little.

They wouldn't help him so instead, I went to the cupboard and pulled out his old pair.

Tatty, falling apart, hole in the sole - but his. Shoes that carried his rhythm, his comfort, his identity.

I handed them to him. Watched him hold them, breathe them in, clutch them like a friend.

Then I took what I could from them - the laces, the soft sticker I'd once added when he told me "The scratchy bit" hurt.

I transplanted those pieces into the new ones. A bridge, not a jump.

I didn't force them on his feet. Didn't say, "Now try."

I just said, "Tomorrow."

And he didn't say no.

That was enough.

◆ ◆ ◆

Maggie's Notes

- New = danger. Old = anchor.

- Shoes hold memory, smell, rhythm.

- Don't say "You'll get used to it." Ever.

- Bridge with safe parts: laces, stickers, textures.

- Tomorrow > today. Let him choose the timing.

◆ ◆ ◆

Between Us

Joe's World

Shoes aren't just shoes. They're memory stitched in leather; rhythm pressed in soles. His old pair weren't rags - they were anchors. New shoes erase that. They're strangers. Even touching them was progress.

Maggie's World

Maggie learns that change can't be forced. She stops herself from the tired phrase - "you'll get used to it" - and builds a bridge instead. Safe laces, soft stickers, gentle tomorrow. She learns that patience isn't weakness. It's wisdom.

(breathing, blanket, colour rules), his deliberate "Maggie" voice, Maggie's apology, shorthand notes, and a more layered *Between Us*.

Narrator's Take

Shoes aren't just shoes.

They're certainty. They hold routines in their soles, comfort in their stitching, and identity in their worn-out creases.

Joe's old shoes were frayed at the ends and the insoles curled like dried leaves. But they fit. Not just his feet - his days. They squeaked when he walked, and the squeak meant "normal." The scuff on the toe meant "school." The worn-down heel meant "safe."

But now, the old shoes are gone. Maggie says they had holes. That his socks got wet. That the teacher mentioned it.

Practical truths don't matter to Joe's nervous system.

What matters is that the new shoes don't squeak.

They feel wrong. They smell wrong. They make him taller in the mirror. The laces are stiffer. The way they bend when he walks feels different. That difference sends a thousand alerts through his brain like static electricity.

In the shop, he touches all the boxes - not out of indecision, but data gathering. The tags scratch. The lights hum. The assistant hovers. There's a sigh from someone in the next aisle. Too much.

Joe grips the shelf. Rocks slightly. His eyes scan the same four shoes again. He's not being fussy. He's trying to survive this sensory onslaught.

Maggie kneels beside him, not rushing, just waiting - letting the moment breathe.

Eventually, he chooses a pair.

Not the most comfortable. But the least offensive.

At home, he wears them for seven minutes. Then off again. Then stares at them from the corner of the room, willing them to become familiar.

They will.

But not today.

CHAPTER 6: THE APPOINTMENT

The Narrator's Take
Developmental Note: Heightened Sensory Vulnerability in Unstructured Public Environments

◆ ◆ ◆

Joe's Take

I didn't want to go.
Maggie said it was just a check-up.
But check-ups mean questions.
And waiting rooms.
And new rooms that smell like rubber gloves and too much breath.
She packed a little snack bag.
Three salted crisps in foil.
One blue sensory ring.
My headphones.
But it wasn't the right bag.
It was her big one.
The one with receipts and tissues and keys that jangle too loud.
The car was too hot.
I asked if we could drive with the windows down.
Maggie said, "They won't go down, love - they're stuck again."
So, the air stayed still, and I stayed stiller.
The surgery had a sign on the door that blinked.
"Please arrive 15 minutes early."

I told Maggie that was silly.
If you come early, it just means you sit longer.
She smiled but didn't answer.
The waiting room was yellow.
Not soft yellow.
Sharp yellow.
Like sour sweets or warning tape.
There was a fan in the corner that kept making a click sound.
I counted seven clicks, then a pause.
Seven clicks. Pause.
Seven clicks. Long pause.
There were chairs with sticky leather seats.
Magazines with curls in the corners.
And a baby crying in its pram.
The baby cried like an alarm.
The kind that stays in your ears after it stops.
Someone's phone went off. A siren ringtone.
Then someone else coughed, and someone else said "bless you,"
and someone else laughed - loud.
Maggie said, "You okay, love?"
I wasn't.
But I nodded.
Then the speaker said:
"Joseph Barker. Dr. Kirmani will see you now."
The voice was too fast.
Maggie said, "Come on, that's us."
But my legs weren't ready.
She stood. I didn't.
So, she held out her hand.
I didn't take it.
But I stood up anyway.
The corridor smelled like soap and old flowers.
Not nice flowers.
The ones that sit too long in a vase and turn the water bad.
Dr. Kirmani smiled and said hello.
I didn't.

He wore a purple shirt.
Purple is usually okay.
But this one had buttons that looked like shiny eyes.
He said, "How are you today?"
Maggie started answering for me.
But he said, "Let's hear from Joe."
That's when my hands started twitching.
My knees went up and down under the chair.
He said, "Do you sleep well, Joe?"
I looked at his pen.
It clicked.
He clicked it again.
Click. Click. Click.
"No," I whispered.
"What time do you usually go to bed?"
I looked at Maggie.
He asked more questions.
About food.
About baths.
About friends.
The word "friends" made my ears feel hot.
The lights were too white.
Too close.
Then a knock on the door.
Another nurse asking about some paper.
I covered my ears.
Then his phone buzzed on the table.
He looked down, mid-sentence.
That's when it happened.
The fuzz took over.
My brain buzzed.
My throat got thick.
The room shrank but the sounds got bigger.
I stood up.
Maggie touched my arm.
Too fast.

Too much.
I pulled away.
I shouted.
Not with words. With noise.
Then I dropped to the floor.
It felt safer there.
Maggie got down beside me.
She didn't tell me off.
She just whispered, "Too much, love. I know. Too much."
And I cried.
Not loud.
But big.
Dr. Kirmani didn't speak.
Not at first.
Then he said, quietly, "I understand. Let's press pause here."

◆ ◆ ◆

Maggie's Take

I should've asked more questions before we came.
Should've called ahead.
Should've warned them.
But I thought… it's just a check-up.
There's no such thing as *just* with Joe.
He was already buzzing in the car.
I could see it.
The way he looked at the window button.
The way he stared at his bag.
I should've known.
When we sat in the waiting room, I wanted to tell the receptionist we needed quiet.
But then you feel like *that* parent.
The fussy one.
The over-anxious one.
And now look.

He was on the floor, clinging to his own knees like they were lifebelts.

The doctor was kind.

He gave us time.

He waited.

He didn't rush.

When Joe calmed down enough to sit again - just on the floor, not the chair - the doctor bent down too.

He said, "Next time, I'll make sure we skip the waiting room.

You come straight in.

Lights off if needed.

No noise.

You tell me."

I nodded, biting my tongue.

He looked at Joe.

"Does that sound okay?"

Joe didn't answer.

But he didn't run.

That's as close to "okay" as we were going to get today.

As we left, Joe touched my sleeve.

Just once.

Soft.

Then he whispered, "Can we go home?"

I said, "Yes."

And we did.

◆ ◆ ◆

Between Us

Joe's Experience

It wasn't about the doctor. It was the *build-up*. The small things that grew into an avalanche - heat, noise, light, questions. Joe's system was already full before it even began.

Maggie's Experience

Appointments feel like simple admin to most. But Maggie learns for Joe, the environment shapes everything. Advocacy isn't being dramatic - it's *necessary*.

Narrator's Take

The waiting room is rarely designed with regulation in mind - not the kind that matters to someone like Joe. Sounds aren't balanced. Smells aren't subtle. And time doesn't follow the routine.

From the moment he enters, Joe's system is under threat. Chairs scrape tile. Phones ring in sharp bursts. Voices layer over each other like static on a detuned radio. Nothing is rhythmic. Nothing is patterned. The environment frays the edges of his tolerance long before he sees the doctor.

Joe doesn't cry. He doesn't lash out. But the clues are there - to anyone looking.

His shoes squeak against the floor, a sound he repeats until he controls it.

He presses the side of his head with his palm, as if trying to push the sound away from inside.

He doesn't sit. He perches.

When Maggie speaks, he doesn't respond. Not because he doesn't hear - but because he can't sift her voice from the noise.

When the consultation finally begins, Joe is already past regulation. A doctor's voice asking questions becomes interrogation. A blood pressure cuff is a restraint. A clipboard is a symbol of being studied, judged, misunderstood.

What Maggie sees is confusion. What Joe experiences is chaos. What the doctor realises - thankfully - is that this isn't defiance or difficulty.

It's overload.

And next time, they promise, things will be different.

This chapter presents a key turning point in Maggie's advocacy and in service response. It marks the beginning of adjustment.

CHAPTER 7: THE WRONG CUP

The Narrators Take
Developmental Note: *Fragility of Safety Through Predictable Objects and Patterns*

◆ ◆ ◆

Maggie's Take - *Regret in Real Time*

The dog was barking. Sharp bursts that bounced off the walls. The kettle was screeching, clicking, hissing like it had a grudge. The post smacked the mat like a slap. My tea had already gone cold before I'd even sat down.

And then Joe asked for the blue cup.

The blue cup was in the dishwasher.

I was tired. My head buzzed, knees aching from yesterday's stairs. My hands smelled faintly of soap. I looked at the sink, looked at him, looked at the green cup waiting on the counter.

So, I said it. Too quick. Too careless.

"Use the green one, Joe. It's just a cup."

He froze. Didn't blink. Didn't breathe. His shoulders stiff, his eyes locked on me.

And I snapped. Not full shout. But sharp. Too sharp.

"I said use the green one!"

The silence after was louder than the kettle.

His eyes dropped. His hands curled tight. He turned. Walked out. Straight up the stairs.

I stood with the green cup in my hand, shaking slightly. The dog barked once more, then stopped. The kettle clicked off. The house fell heavy.

I'd done the thing I swore I wouldn't. Not to him. Not like that.

◆ ◆ ◆

Joe's Take- *This Cup Doesn't Belong*

It's not about the cup.

It's never about the cup.

It's about knowing. About the rhythm. The beat. The dance. Cups, spoons, seats, doors - each keeps time.

Maggie broke the dance.

Her voice was a crack. Sudden, sharp, splintery. Like glass under my shoes.

My chest went tight. My breath stopped. My hands twitched but I didn't flap.

I didn't argue. That makes it worse.

I didn't cry. That draws eyes.

I didn't shout. That breaks rules.

I left.

Upstairs. Blanket. Heavy one. Blue-grey, weight pressed into my skin. Heavy means calm. Weight pins me in place, makes my body real.

I shut my eyes. Shapes came anyway. Jagged. Red. Sharp edges cutting through the dark.

The cup is blue. Not just blue - mine. Fits my hands. Smooth where the sticker wore off. Doesn't smell like soap. Always ready when I am.

Dad never shouted about cups.

He just knew.

◆ ◆ ◆

Maggie's Take

I didn't follow. Didn't rush. Didn't throw more noise into his silence.

I washed the blue cup. Slow. Careful. Like crystal. Dried it until no drop clung. Held it in the same hand that had gripped the green one minutes before. The weight the same. The meaning worlds apart.

I walked to his door. Stood still. My hand hovered, tempted to knock. But knocking would be intrusion.

So, I spoke. Soft.

"The blue cup's clean now. And I shouldn't have shouted. I'm sorry."

I set it on the floor outside. A peace offering. A flag between us.

Then I went back down. Sat at the table. Waited. The kettle quiet. The house breathing again.

◆ ◆ ◆

Joe's Part

The house felt quiet. Too quiet.

I waited under my blanket. Breathed in fours.

In. Two, three, four.

Out. Two, three, four.

Opened one eye. The door was still shut.

Opened the other. Then opened the door.

The cup was there.

Blue. Clean. Dry. Mine.

I picked it up. Ran my thumb over the smooth patch where the sticker used to be. The cup fit my hands like always.

I went downstairs.

Didn't look at her. Just sat. Poured juice. Took one sip.

Then I said, "Don't be like other people."

Maggie smiled. Tired, but real.

"I'm trying, kid. I really am."

◆ ◆ ◆

Maggie's Notes

- Cups = signals. Wrong cup = broken rhythm.

- "It's just..." = dangerous words. Never minimise.

- Raised voice = cracks the whole day.

- Heavy blanket = reset tool. Respect it.

- Peace offering works better than chasing.

- Apology should be quiet, simple, honest.

◆ ◆ ◆

Between Us

Joe's World
The blue cup isn't preference. It's proof. Proof that the rhythm is intact. The wrong cup shatters it. His retreat upstairs wasn't sulk. It was survival. His blanket, his breathing, his silence - his way to reset.

Maggie's World
Maggie snapped. She slipped. But the repair mattered more than the mistake. She didn't chase him. Didn't drown him in words. She placed the blue cup, offered an apology, and waited. Trust isn't kept by being perfect. It's kept by repairing gently when you fail.

The Narrators Take

Sometimes, safety doesn't look like a locked door or a hand to hold. Sometimes, it looks like a cup - the cup.
Green, smooth-rimmed, always dry. The one thing that doesn't surprise you when your skin is already crawling with too much sound, too much smell, too many questions in your head.
Joe's world isn't built on what's big. It's built on what's known.

When the cup changes, the ground beneath him shifts.

The behaviour is subtle - at first.

He stares too long at the object.

His shoulders rise but don't drop.

His hands curl, then flap once - a premature burst of internal pressure escaping.

When Maggie speaks, her tone - just a little too fast, a little too firm - hits like static.

That's when he shouts.

That's when the cup crashes.

But that moment isn't about disrespect. It's not a tantrum.

It's grief for lost control.

Maggie's snap - fast and accidental - slices through him.

And in the echo, silence wins. Joe retreats.

Maggie sees it too late.

This is the cost of a single oversight when the world is already heavy. But it's also the chapter where both begin to recover differently.

Maggie doesn't chase him up the stairs.

Joe doesn't lock the door.

There's pain. But there's also pause - a space to start again.

CHAPTER 8: RED COAT DAY

The Narrators Take
Developmental Note: Autonomy, Identity, and the Power Struggle of Perceived Control

◆ ◆ ◆

Joe's Take - Too Bright, Too Loud, Too Wrong

The red coat is bad.

It smells like the shop. Plastic bags, glue, cardboard, other people's hands. Not my smell. Not safe.

My coat - the blue one - has soft sleeves. Rubbed down at the cuffs where I twist them when I'm waiting. A secret hole in the pocket where I keep folded bus tickets. It bends with me. It understands me.

But today Maggie held up the red coat.

She said the zip on the blue one broke. Said it was "too far gone." She smiled like it was a joke. But coats aren't jokes. Coats are rules. I stepped back. My heels hit the skirting. I counted the floor tiles. One, two, three, four, five, six. Counting pins the room down. My finger brushed the radiator. Once. Twice. Three. Four. Four makes balance.

Then I hummed my safe song. The space cartoon theme. Low, buzzing in my throat, steady as a rope to hold.

Maggie crouched. Her knees clicked. She said, "It's warm. It's soft. It's just a coat, Joe."

But it wasn't just anything.

It was red.

Red means stop. Red means alarm. Red means too much.

I didn't scream. I didn't run.

I went flat.

Flat is when your body drops without asking.

Flat is when your arms feel like sandbags.

Flat is when the world spins, so you lie down to hold it still.

I lay on the carpet. Cold fibres against my cheek. Smell of dust in my nose. Eyes closed. Breathing like the sea.

In. Two, three, four.

Out. Two, three, four.

She didn't talk. She just sat.

And after a while, she put the red coat next to me. Not on me. Not touching. Just near.

I didn't wear it that day.

But I let her carry it.

That's something.

◆ ◆ ◆

Maggie's Take - *Stuck in the Storm*

The zip was gone. Split, jagged, impossible to fix.

I thought I was being kind. Thought I was solving a problem. Bringing home a brand-new coat - thick, soft, padded. Red like Christmas berries. I imagined him smiling, burying his hands into the lining.

I forgot about red.

I forgot what his coat really was. Not just warmth. Not just fabric. Memory. Familiarity. The smell of playgrounds, the rhythm of school runs, the touch of his own hands twisting the sleeves.

The moment he saw the red, he dropped. Not tantrum. Not fight. Just flat. His body folding in on itself like someone had cut the strings.

Every part of me wanted to fix it. To say, "It's fine. It's just a coat.

Just a colour."
But I stopped myself. I remembered. Don't argue him out of how he feels. Meet him where he is.
So, I sat.
I didn't force. Didn't beg. Didn't push.
After a while, I placed it beside him. Quietly. Not a demand. Just a possibility.
He didn't wear it.
But when I asked, "Can I bring it?" he nodded. Quick. Definite.
And that was enough.

❖ ❖ ❖

Maggie's Notes

- Red = alarm. Too loud. Too much.

- Old coat = memory, rhythm, safety.

- Flat ≠ lazy. Flat = survival pause.

- Don't say "It's just…" about anything.

- Don't force. Sit. Wait. Offer quietly.

- Carrying it = step one.

❖ ❖ ❖

Between Us

Joe's World

Colours aren't decoration. They're signals. Red doesn't just stand out. It shouts. His blue coat wasn't tatters. It was trust. Losing it felt like losing armour. Going flat wasn't defiance. It was survival - pressing pause until the storm passed.

Maggie's World

Maggie learns that her instinct to persuade would break him further. By sitting, waiting, and placing the coat nearby, she gave Joe choice. Trust isn't built by force. It's built by patience. Sometimes the bravest act is letting go of control.

The Narrators Take

The coat wasn't about colour.
Not really.
It was about choice. About being seen, heard, and respected - even in the smallest decisions.
When Joe says "no," it's not just resistance. It's expression.
Red is too loud. Too bright. Too tight in the wrong places.
It screams when he wants to whisper.
To Maggie, it was just a coat. To Joe, it was a threat to his autonomy.
And that's the collision.
What professionals often label as "defiance" might just be a child shouting, "This is too much, and no one's listening."
The behaviours tell us more than words ever could:
Joe stalls at the doorway.
Avoids eye contact.
Begins scripting, softly at first, then louder.
Repeats yesterday's routine - a desperate attempt to rewind the present.
Flaps - not as release, but as shield.
And when the coat goes on anyway?
It doesn't just cling to his skin.
It erases his say.
Maggie sees it in his posture before she hears the crack in his voice. And when she finally hears the words - "I said no!" - she realises what they cost him to say.
This chapter isn't about a piece of clothing.
It's about a line being drawn in the sand - and how trust, once crossed, takes longer to rebuild than it did to break.

But rebuild it, they will.
Because later, Maggie leaves the red coat folded on the chair.
And Joe walks past it - untouched but unafraid.
That's growth.

CHAPTER 9: A NEW SOUND

The Narrators Take

Developmental Note: Regulating Through Routine – Introducing Tools for Self-Soothing

◆ ◆ ◆

Maggie's Take - *Better Doesn't Always Mean Better*

I bought him new headphones.

Proper ones. Big, padded, noise-cancelling. Not the crackly old foam pair he'd been patching with masking tape for weeks. His old ones had tape across the band like a stitched wound. I thought I was doing a good thing.

I thought he'd be excited.

He wasn't.

As soon as he saw the box, he stepped back. Like it buzzed. His eyes darted to the side; his breath went fast.

"Try them," I said. "Just for a minute. You'll love the sound."

He shook his head. Hard.

I wanted to explain - how expensive they were, how many reviews I'd read, how these were *better* than what he had. But then I looked at his face.

It said: *This isn't help. This is change.*

So, I shut my mouth.

◆ ◆ ◆

Take - *It's Not Broken, It's Not Mine*

They were black. Too black. Shiny in patches, dull in others. The box smelled like plastic and electricity.

My old headphones hum when I wear them. Soft buzz. Steady. They hum like my heart.

The new ones were too quiet. Silence isn't always safe. Silence can be like falling.

I touched them once. Just one finger. Cold. Hard. The padding thick like a pillow stuffed too much. Wrong.

I sniffed them. Not sweat, not leather. Just factory.

Maggie said, "They'll help."

But help isn't loud. Help listens first.

My chest started the fast breath. In. In. In. I hummed under my breath to steady it. My safe song. The space cartoon theme. The buzz in my throat anchored me.

I placed the headphones down. Carefully. Gently. Not a throw. Not anger.

"I can't today," I said.

And Maggie didn't make me.

◆ ◆ ◆

Maggie's Take

He put them down. Didn't break them. Didn't shout. Just said no.

And I nodded. "Okay."

And I meant it.

For once, I didn't argue. Didn't guilt him about money. Didn't beg for him to just try.

Later that night, when the dog finally stopped shifting in its basket and the house went still, I placed the new headphones in his drawer. Not hidden. Just waiting. Neat beside the charger.

On top, I left a note in thick pen:

If you ever change your mind, they're here.

Not pressure. Not force. Just invitation.

He hasn't touched them yet.

But yesterday, I caught him looking. His eyes lingered a second too long before darting away.

That's enough.

◆ ◆ ◆

Maggie's Notes

- Old = hum = safe. New = silence = falling.

- Smell matters. Plastic = wrong. Familiar = safe.

- Help = listening, not persuading.

- "Not today" = full sentence. Respect it.

- Keep choices visible, not hidden.

◆ ◆ ◆

Between Us

Joe's World

Old headphones aren't rubbish. They're armour. They hum like his heartbeat. The new pair, though technically better, are strangers. Too quiet. Too new. Saying "I can't today" wasn't rejection. It was honesty. And readiness can't be rushed.

Maggie's World

Maggie learns that giving isn't about price tags or research. It's about timing and choice. By not pushing, by letting no mean no, she gave Joe control. Leaving the headphones visible turned them from a threat into a possibility.

The Narrators Take

There are sounds you can't escape.

Some come from inside - the thud of your own heartbeat, the fizz in your blood when the world turns too fast.

Others creep in from outside - sharp voices, scraping chairs, ticking clocks that feel like thunder.

For Joe, sound isn't background.

It's centre-stage.

He doesn't hear it. He feels it.

And that feeling can be too much.

The old headphones were patched up. Fraying.

They weren't perfect, but they were familiar. They shaped the world just enough.

They carried the memory of safer mornings.

So, when Maggie brings new ones - clean, crisp, black, whole - it's not just an upgrade.

It's an unknown.

Transitions like this aren't about things. They're about certainty.

The unspoken panic sounds like silence at first.

Then comes the pacing. The scanning.

The pause before touching.

The hesitation before trust.

Professionals might call it "rigidity."

But really, it's grief.

Mourning the loss of something that helped him feel safe - and fearing the new won't do the same.

But then Joe listens.

One beat at a time.

The outside world becomes dimmer, not gone - just less sharp.

And for the first time in days, he hums again.

It's not the sound of the headphones.

It's the sound of relief.

CHAPTER 10: THE LIST

The Narrators Take
Developmental Note: Planning as Emotional Regulation – When Control Becomes Comfort

◆ ◆ ◆

Joe's Take - *The List is the Law*

Maggie lost the list.
Not just any list.
The list.
My list.
The one I wrote in green pen. Green is safe. Not red (alarm). Not black (tests). Green is calm.
I'd drawn ticks for the things already done. Circles for what was next. Circles mean *not yet*. Ticks mean *safe*.
We were going to town. I had it ready:

•   Bus at 10:32 (front seat if available).

•   Walk past the fountain (no coins in it).

•   Library for map book (no talking).

•   Quiet café. Booth. Right-hand wall.

•   Back by 12:47.

That's the route. That's the rule.

But Maggie left the paper on the counter. She said, "It's fine, Joe. You remember it anyway."

But remembering isn't the same as seeing.

My brain scrambles the steps if I don't see them. Scrambles like eggs. Messy. Hot. Slipping everywhere.

I stopped walking. Outside the bus stop.

My breath did the fast thing.

In. In. In.

No out.

My hand curled into a claw. My thigh tapped. My rucksack strap cut into my shoulder. I stared at the ground, grey slabs with cracks. If I looked up, the sky might tip me.

Maggie crouched. Close enough for her shadow to brush mine. Not touching. Not pushing.

She held out a pen. And her hand.

"Tell me the list," she said. "We'll make a new one. Together."

Her voice was steady.

So, I told her. One step at a time. Bricks laid back down.

She wrote them. In green pen. She knew.

I took the pen. Underlined it twice. Hard. Firm. Restored.

My chest loosened. Finally.

We got on the bus.

◆ ◆ ◆

Maggie's Take - *Trying to Catch Up*

It was my fault. The list was on the counter, half under the post. I'd meant to grab it. I didn't.

I thought, *He'll remember it. He's sharp. He's got it in his head.*

But this wasn't memory. It was certainty. Without the paper, he froze. Not tantrum. Not stubbornness. Frozen wires.

He stopped outside the stop. Shoulders locked. Breathing too fast. I didn't say, "It's fine." I didn't tell him I knew it. My knowing wasn't enough. He needed to see it.

So, I crouched. Pen in hand. Palm open.

"Tell me the list," I said. "We'll make a new one. Together."

He gave me the steps, one by one, like testing me. I wrote them exactly. His words, not mine.

When he took the pen and underlined it, I knew. We'd repaired what I'd broken. And we carried on.

◆ ◆ ◆

Maggie's Notes

- Lists = lifelines. Seeing > remembering.

- Green pen = calm. Never swap colour.

- Freeze ≠ stubborn. Freeze = survival.

- Don't say "It's fine." Say "Let's write it."

- Repair fast. Don't defend. Rebuild.

◆ ◆ ◆

Between Us

Joe's World

Lists aren't reminders. They're anchors. Ticks and circles aren't decoration - they're proof the world is safe. Without the list, everything scrambles. His fast breathing, his claw hand, his stillness - all signals. Making a new list wasn't a workaround. It was repair.

Maggie's World

Maggie slipped. But she didn't argue, defend, or minimise. She adapted. Wrote his steps, his way, his colour. Repair was quicker than reassurance. By listening and writing, she turned a broken start into a saved day.

The Narrators Take

Sometimes the world makes no sense -
so, Joe writes it down.
Lists aren't just reminders.
They're anchors.
Each item is a promise. A step. A map through the chaos.
He doesn't write in loops or flourish.
He writes in straight lines.
One item. One truth. One thing he can control.
This list? It's about pancakes.
But it's also about knowing what's coming.
Because what if the eggs are gone?
What if Maggie forgets the syrup?
What if the shop smells like bleach again?
When you don't get to choose the noise, the smell, the flicker of
overhead lights,
you choose the order.
You choose the pencil.
You choose the words.
That's not rigidity.
That's resilience.
Maggie sees the list.
She sees more than a shopping note -
She sees trust.
Because Joe is letting her in, one written instruction at a time.
If the world is loud, and your body won't stop fizzing, and the
smell of oranges can ruin your day-
then knowing that syrup is number three on the list might be the
only thing that saves you.

CHAPTER 11: THE DAY WITHOUT MAGGIE

The Narrators Take

Developmental Note: Disrupted Attachment – The Impact of Unexpected Change on Felt Safety

◆ ◆ ◆

Joe's Take

The hallway smelled different.
No toast. No lavender hand cream.
Just aftershave. Sharp and cold.
I looked out of my window at 8:01.
The car wasn't there.
Maggie always parks in the same spot - under the tall tree with the droopy branch.
It was empty.
I asked, "Where's Maggie?"
The man said, "She's just out, mate. I'm here today."
He smiled like he was being helpful.
I didn't smile back.
I sat on the stairs.
Counted the bars on the railing.
Felt the air change.
The house echoed.
Too loud.
Too quiet.

The man said, "I'm your Uncle Dave. You remember me, right?"
I didn't.
Or maybe I did once. But today I didn't.
He moved differently.
Spoke too fast.
Touched things too much.
He opened the fridge.
Used the *wrong* cup.
Turned the *wrong* light on.
Opened *both* curtains.
I told him the telly goes on at 10:15.
He turned it on at 9:43.
"Little early treat," he said.
But it wasn't a treat.
It was a crack in the routine.
My skin felt prickly.
I rocked forward and back.
Uncle Dave said, "You alright, champ?"
I wasn't a champ.
I was a storm.
I didn't eat lunch.
He tried. Sandwiches. Crisps.
Even jelly.
But he used the red plate.
The red plate means no.
Emergency. Danger. Don't.
I sat in the hallway.
Waited.
Checked the clock every 12 minutes.
Waited.
Listened.
Waited.
Then the key in the door.
Maggie.
Hair a bit messy.
Smelled like rain and tired.

She said, "I'm sorry, love. Got held up."
I didn't answer.
I just walked to the corner of the room.
Pressed my hands against the wall.
Maggie didn't ask for a hug.
She didn't say anything for a bit.
Then she said, "Was it hard?"
I nodded.
She said, "Me too."

◆ ◆ ◆

Maggie's Take

It was just a training day.
A short session.
Safeguarding, they said. Mandatory.
I left a full note.
Laid everything out.
Joe's snacks.
Timings.
Instructions.
What not to say.
What *never* to do.
Dave's good. He means well.
But he's not me.
And more importantly, he's not *familiar*.
The moment I got out of training, I checked my phone - four missed calls.
None from Joe.
But still, it made my chest ache.
I rushed home.
Rain on my coat.
Shoes soaked.
Opened the door, saw Joe - small and curled, like a bracket.
I knew.

He'd held it all day.
And now I was back, it was safe to let go.
I told him I was sorry.
I didn't over-explain.
I just said, "Me too."
And we sat.
No telly.
No talk.
Just a shared quiet.
Sometimes that's all a person needs to feel whole again.

◆ ◆ ◆

Between Us

Joe's Experience

Familiarity is safety. Maggie's absence felt like a betrayal - not because she did anything wrong, but because his world depends on *knowing*. Uncle Dave broke the rules Joe lives by - even if he didn't mean to.

Maggie's Experience

Even short gaps in care are big events in Joe's world. Maggie learns that even with prep, some days will feel like a storm - and returning quietly, gently, and with honesty is the best shelter she can offer.

The Narrators Take

Every routine has a rhythm.
Every rhythm holds a person.
And when that person doesn't appear -
even for a little while -
the whole song goes quiet.
Joe's world isn't built on trust that people stay.
It's built on patterns that people sometimes stay... until they don't.

He doesn't ask, "Where is she?"

He asks, "Is she coming back?"

But not out loud.

Out loud, he asks nothing.

The new adult smells different. Talks different. Makes the wrong noise when they laugh.

They speak like they've met Joe before, but their voice isn't in his memory.

They put the wrong show on. Too loud.

They offer food at the wrong time. Too soon.

Joe copes - in his way.

Counting. Pacing. Watching the clock. Pressing his ear to the window.

The silence inside him grows louder than the sound outside.

Maggie's delay wasn't long.

But for Joe, it wasn't minutes that mattered. It was certainty.

And that certainty vanished the moment the doorbell rang, and it wasn't her.

When she finally returns -

her breath rushed, her keys jangling -

she doesn't realise right away that Joe's not upset with her.

He's upset with everything that came instead.

Because when you've lost people before,

every new goodbye sounds permanent.

CHAPTER 12: THE WRONG WORDS

The Narrators Take

Developmental Note: Emotional Regulation – When Language Triggers a Fight or Flight Response

◆ ◆ ◆

Maggie's Take - *Learning the Real Language*

It started with a joke.

At least, I thought it was a joke.

Beans on toast. One of the few meals I can manage without second-guessing myself. Joe likes them a certain way - beans drained, toast cold, never overlapping. I've learned that much.

But I was tired. My back ached, my head felt heavy. I sighed.

And I said it.

"You're a right little fusspot, aren't you?"

It slipped out. Light, casual, the kind of thing you say without thinking. No malice. Just a filler word.

But the fork stopped mid-air.

His eyes went still. No blink. No breath.

He put the fork down. Quiet. Deliberate. Like a switch being flipped.

Then he left the table.

No flapping. No tantrum. No sound.

Just gone.

I stared at the empty seat.

And I knew.
I'd broken something.

◆ ◆ ◆

Joe's Take - *Say it Right, or Don't Say It*

Fusspot.
I don't know what that word means.
But it felt sharp. Like a needle behind my eyes.
I was eating the beans the right way. The safe way. Toast cold.
Beans drained. Fork steady. Each bite lined up in order. Nothing
touching.
Maggie's voice didn't fit her face. Her mouth smiled, but it wasn't
soft. It curled. Crooked. Her voice was light, but it had splinters
inside. Splinters catch. Splinters hurt.
My tummy twisted. The beans turned heavy, like stones sliding
down.
The fork felt wrong in my hand. Metal too cold, edge too sharp.
The scrape against the plate echoed, shrill and scratchy, like chalk
dragged across a board.
Her word echoed too.
Fusspot.
Fusspot.
Fusspot.
Like a drumbeat stuck in my skull.
My chest buzzed. Breath jammed. My ears rang, filling with white
hiss. The ceiling lights flickered too loud, their hum turning to
needles in my head.
So, I left.
Not running. Not shouting. Not flapping. Just leaving. Quiet,
deliberate, heavy steps. Each one felt like pushing through mud.
I went to my corner. My whale blanket. Blue, with faded fins
stitched across. The only blue still mine that day.
I pulled it over my head. Fabric pressing down, weight turning
panic into something solid.

At first, my breathing stuttered.

In. In. In.

No out.

Then I counted. Ninety-nine. Twice. Numbers build order. Words only scramble.

I hummed. My cartoon theme. The buzz in my throat replaced the word in my head. Slowly. Not gone. But smaller.

I stayed under until the splinter dulled. Until "fusspot" was only an echo, not a shout.

She didn't follow.

Not at first.

◆ ◆ ◆

Maggie's Take

I waited. Ten minutes, maybe more. Long enough for my tea to cool, for the clock to tick too loudly in the kitchen.

Then I went.

He was in the corner, blanket fort built around himself, like a turtle in its shell. Just the faintest hum from inside - his cartoon theme tune. Steady, low, protective.

I didn't pull the blanket. Didn't peek. I just sat down next to it. Cross-legged. Close enough for him to hear me breathe.

After a while, I said, "That word upset you."

The blanket twitched. Just a ripple.

So, I tried again. "I'm learning too."

Silence.

I didn't push more words. Just stayed. My knees went numb, but I stayed.

Later that night, when the house was still, I found a folded scrap of paper on the counter.

His handwriting. Green pen. Blocky, square.

Fusspot is not funny. Beans are not bad. Please don't laugh at safe things.

I've kept it. Folded into my wallet. Tucked next to his school photo.

A reminder. A promise not to forget.

❖ ❖ ❖

Maggie's Notes

- Words = weight. Even "jokes" land sharp.

- Safe routines = untouchable. Don't laugh at them.

- Silence = signal. Respect it.

- Blanket + counting = reset zone. Let it be.

- Notes = his language. Keep them safe.

-

❖ ❖ ❖

Between Us

Joe's World
Words aren't decoration. They cut, they soothe, they shape. Even when dressed as jokes, they can splinter safety. Beans and toast weren't fussiness. They were certainty. Her word bent that certainty, so he bent away - silent, shielded, under his blanket, counting and humming until the sting shrank.

Maggie's World
Maggie learned that language carries more weight than she realised. Her apology wasn't words but listening. Waiting. Accepting his note as truth. Keeping it in her wallet turned it from paper into promise. She'll carry it like a shield to remind her: safety is never a joke.

The Narrators Take

Words are not just sounds.

For some, they are landmines.
Small syllables that explode without warning.
"You're being silly."
"It's not a big deal."
"Calm down."
Wrong words. All of them.
They don't calm. They don't explain.
They don't help.
They poke at the most sensitive part of the brain - the one that hears danger even when danger isn't there.
They override logic. Replace safety with shame.
Joe doesn't hear Maggie's intent.
He hears rejection.
He hears misunderstanding.
He hears every adult who ever got it wrong before.
And his nervous system doesn't pause to check.
It acts.
Fight. Flight. Or freeze.
He lashes out - not to hurt, but to release.
Not to punish, but to communicate the only way his overwhelmed mind can manage.
And Maggie?
Maggie stays.
Not frozen. Not angry.
She lowers her voice, her posture, her energy.
Because the wrong words have already been spoken.
And now the only language that matters is presence.

CHAPTER 13: THE INVITATION

The Narrators Take
Developmental Note: Social Exposure – Anticipation, Uncertainty, and the Weight of "Maybe"

◆ ◆ ◆

Joe's Take

The envelope was orange.
Orange is not a safe colour. Orange means loud. Like traffic cones. Or fire drills. Or the shirt my dad wore when he painted the shed and dropped the tin.
I didn't open it.
Maggie did. She read it out loud in her "excited" voice. The one with rounded edges.
"You've been invited to Zach's birthday party!"
I knew Zach. He sat four chairs away in school. He always had stickers on his jumper and one long eyebrow that didn't stop.
I didn't talk to him. He once asked me if I liked slime. I didn't answer.
Maggie read more. "There'll be cake, music, dancing, a magician-"
I closed my ears. Not with my hands. With my mind. Like pressing a cushion hard against a window to block the cold in winter.
The party was Saturday. That was tomorrow.
She said, "Only if you want to, love."
I didn't say yes. I didn't say no.

Instead, I made a plan.

I watched three party videos on the iPad. I paused them and wrote down the steps in order: balloons, cake, hats, pass the parcel, presents, noise.

I packed my bag:

- Ear defenders

- Blue visor (just in case)

- Green towel (for pressure comfort)

- One cereal bar, chocolate chip only

- Two battery packs for the iPad

- A note that said, "Joe needs quiet now" (in case I couldn't speak)

I laid out my clothes: soft blue top, no seams; joggers with no tags; socks inside out; trainers with the left foot done first.

I practiced smiling in the mirror. It made my cheeks hurt.

The hall smelled of jelly. And bleach. And feet.

Children ran in loops. Loud ones. Their shoes slapped the floor like wet towels.

Zach's mum wore sequins that flashed too bright. She waved at me.

"Hi Joe! So glad you could make it!"

Her voice was bells. I wanted to say, *please talk quieter.* But I didn't.

I walked along the edge. One foot balanced on the skirting board line. One finger trailing the wall. That helped.

Then it happened.

A balloon burst.

The sound was sharp, instant, like a slap next to my head. My body jolted. My legs stopped working properly.

I crouched, like a spring wound tight, but I didn't bounce. My hands pressed to my ears. Not fast. Just enough to push the world away.

The smell of rubber hit me next. Burnt and sour.

Then Zach's dad appeared. Big man. Big voice. "Hey buddy! Want a turn at the game?"

He high fived the air. Too close. His hand swiped the space in front of me like a net.

I didn't want to touch it. Or him. Or speak. Or nod.

He stepped closer.

So, I ran.

Through the kitchen. Past the coats. To the fire door with the red light above.

Maggie was already there.

She opened her arms, but didn't touch me.

I slid down the wall beside her. My breath rattled.

She said nothing.

That was good.

We sat for six minutes and thirty-four seconds. I counted. Numbers fix the cracks.

Then I said, "Can we go?"

And she said, "Yes."

That was better.

We got home and I sat on the beanbag.

Not under the blanket. Just on it. That's how you know I wasn't broken. Just bent.

Maggie brought toast. Two slices. Corner-to-corner.

She sat on the floor next to me.

"I'm proud of you, y'know."

I blinked once.

"Not for staying. For trying."

"But I left," I said.

"You also showed up."

I looked at the crust of the toast.

"Was it wrong to run?"

"No," she said. "It was right to listen to yourself."

I stared at the floor. "Why do other kids not run?"

"They've had more practice," she said. "And their heads don't get

as full as fast."
I picked up the toast. Took one bite.
"Will I go again?"
"Maybe," she said. "Maybe not."
And then she said the best thing.
"We go at your speed, boss."
That made me feel bigger inside.
Like I was finally catching up to something.

◆ ◆ ◆

Maggie's Take

The ride home was quiet.
No tears. No fight. Just Joe twisting the hoodie strings in his fingers like dials, turning them until they nearly knotted.
I made toast. His way.
He sat on the beanbag, still in his shoes, still with his bag nearby.
His anchor, just in case.
I sat beside him, on the floor where he prefers me. Level, not towering.
"I'm proud of you, y'know," I said.
He blinked, surprised.
"Not for staying. For trying."
"But I left," he said.
"You also showed up."
His shoulders softened, just slightly.
"Was it wrong to run?" he asked.
"No," I said. "It was right to listen to yourself."
And then I saw it - the flicker. The one that means he's absorbing it, not just hearing.
So, I told him: "We go at your speed, boss."
He didn't smile. But he finished his toast.
That was enough.

◆ ◆ ◆

Maggie's Notes

- Orange = loud, unsafe.

- Preparation = armour. Bag, clothes, lists. Respect it.

- Edges of rooms = safety lines.

- Balloon burst = overload trigger. Watch for crouch + ears covered.

- Running = coping, not failing.

- Praise the trying, not the staying.

◆ ◆ ◆

Between Us

Joe's World

Parties aren't fun. They're puzzles made of noise, smells, lights, and rules that keep shifting. Every balloon is a threat. Every cheer is a bang. Preparing isn't fussiness - it's survival. Running wasn't giving up. It was listening to his body.

Maggie's World

Maggie didn't force him to stay to prove a point. She counted effort as victory. She didn't fix the moment. She sat inside it. She gave praise not for endurance, but for bravery. By calling him "boss," she shifted the power back into his hands.

The Narrators Take

It's just a piece of paper to most.
A fold, a scribble, a time, a place.
But for some, it's a question with no answer.
"Will I be okay there?"
"What if it's loud?"

"What if there's cake I don't like?"
"What if I say the wrong thing?"
"What if I don't know the rules?"
The invitation isn't exciting.
It's terrifying.
Because it doesn't just ask you to come -
It asks you to cope.
With people.
With noise.
With expectation.
It puts the spotlight on social scripts you never rehearsed.
It demands unspoken codes you never got a copy of.
It says, "Join us," but forgets to say how.
Joe doesn't see a party.
He sees potential chaos.
He hears echoes before they happen.
And Maggie?
She sees hope. A chance. A step forward.
But she also sees the tight shoulders, the hesitation, the barely-there nod.
They both read the same card -
But only one sees how far the distance is between the envelope and the door.

CHAPTER 14: PANCAKE TUESDAY

The Narrators Take
Developmental Note: Co-Regulation Through Shared Activity – Tactile Bonding, Anticipation, and Unspoken Repair

◆ ◆ ◆

Joe's Take - *Too Much Flip, Not Enough Order*

Pancake Tuesday is not about pancakes.

It's about the order of things.

First, I get the mixing bowl from the low cupboard. It has a chip on the side shaped like a triangle. My fingers fit the groove. That means it's the right bowl.

Then I check the eggs. They must be brown. Not white. White is wrong. White is hospital. White is cold hands.

Then I stand by the counter and listen to the milk jug. When the bubbles rise and pop, it makes a sound like a soft cough.

That tells me the milk is warm enough.

Mum used to flip the pancake at 7:43 exactly. She didn't need a clock. I always checked anyway.

Maggie tried at 7:50.

Too late.

Too wrong.

The numbers didn't line up. The rhythm broke.

She also added lemon. Without asking.

Lemon is acid.

Lemon is surprise.

Lemon is not routine.

The smell hit first. Sharp. Sour. It curled in my nose and scratched the back of my throat.

Then the pan hissed. Loud. The butter burned at the edges and spat. The sound was fireworks trapped in a room.

My hands shot to my ears. Pressed tight. Not because she shouted. Because the world did.

The word *lemon* repeated in my head. Over and over.

Lemon.

Lemon.

Lemon.

It filled the space until there was no room for pancakes anymore.

I didn't shout. I didn't argue. I just left.

Empty, not angry.

I sat on the stairs. Socks on. Penguin socks. The ones with little bobbles worn flat at the heels. I pressed my toes into the carpet. Felt the rough weave. Counted the tufts.

And thought about syrup.

Safe syrup.

Sweet. Thick. Predictable.

No lemon.

◆ ◆ ◆

Maggie's Take - *Sweet Doesn't Always Mean Simple*

I thought I was doing a good thing.

Pancake Tuesday. A little celebration. Something normal.

But I was five minutes off schedule. And I forgot the syrup.

Worse - I added lemon. Without asking. Because that's how I've always done it.

I didn't think. Habit took over.

The look on his face wasn't anger. It was worse. It was blank. Like I'd erased something important. Like a page of him had been smudged.

He left without a word.

I wanted to call him back, to explain, to tell him lemon was tradition. But I stopped myself. My tradition isn't his.

So, I stayed put. I cleaned the pan. I turned off the extractor fan. I took off the apron with the grease mark that never comes out. I made the kitchen quiet again.

Then I went to him.

He was on the stairs. Sitting small, his knees pulled in, hands holding his feet like they were glass. Protecting them. Steadying himself.

I didn't launch in with words. I just sat. Close enough. Quiet.

The clock ticked once. Twice.

Then I whispered, "Next Tuesday. Syrup only. You flip."

He didn't nod. He didn't speak.

But he didn't move away.

That's a maybe.

And maybe is enough.

◆ ◆ ◆

Maggie's Notes

- Pancakes = ritual. Not food, but memory.

- Exact times matter. 7:43 ≠ 7:50.

- Lemon = acid = wrong. Syrup = safe.

- Noise of pan = overload trigger. Watch for ears covered.

- Sitting small ≠ ignoring. It's reset.

- Offering control = repair.

◆ ◆ ◆

Between Us

Joe's World
Pancakes aren't about flavour. They're memory stitched into routine. The right bowl, the right eggs, the right time - all anchors. Lemon wasn't a taste. It was a disruption. His silence and leaving weren't defiance. They were survival when the rhythm snapped.

Maggie's World
Maggie acted from habit, not thought. Her intentions were good. But intentions don't erase impact. By turning off the noise, stepping back, and offering him control next time, she showed that repair can be empowerment. Sometimes "maybe" is the best trust she'll get - and that's enough.

The Narrators Take

Some rituals aren't in the rulebook.
They rise from mess. From batter that splashes too far. From silence that cracks like an egg into a hot pan.
Pancake Tuesday doesn't come with instructions.
But for Joe and Maggie, it arrives like a truce wrapped in sugar.
There are no scripts here.
No perfect flips or timed applause.
Just the rhythm of a whisk, the scent of warm vanilla, the stick-slick of syrup trailing down fingers.
Cooking, in moments like this, is not about food.
It's about pace.
It's about joining a task where no one has to look each other in the eye to feel seen.
It's one of the few places where Maggie doesn't push and Joe doesn't flinch.
Where mess is part of the plan.
Maggie watches every sprinkle; listens to every word Joe doesn't say.
She doesn't ask him to say sorry.
She lets him show it instead - in careful measuring, in how he lets

her spread the butter this time.

Joe doesn't need to understand Pancake Tuesday's origin.

He understands what it is now:

A moment where things feel back in place.

CHAPTER 15: THE FIRE DRILL

The Narrators Take

Developmental Note: Sensory Overload and Emotional Recall – The Importance of Predictability and Trauma-Aware Response

◆ ◆ ◆

Joe's Take - *Alarm, Alarm, Alarm*

The lights blinked once. Then again.

Then the sound started.

The alarm was red and spinning. It screamed like a giant bird trapped in a cage. High, sharp, endless.

Everyone moved. Fast. Too fast. Chairs scraped back, a hundred metal claws screeching the floor. Shoes stomped. Bags swung. People shouted - not angry, but loud. Too loud.

I covered my ears. But the noise got in anyway. Like needles sliding through the gaps in my fingers.

Miss Langton touched my arm. I pulled away. Her perfume was peach. Sweet, sticky, heavy. It clung to my nose and throat like glue.

She bent down, voice close. "We have to go, Joe."

But I couldn't.

My feet weren't cold. They were stuck. Poured in cement.

Children passed me. Too close. Brushing my coat. My sleeve.

My hair. The air behind them dragged across my skin like sandpaper.

I tried to find the corner. Corners are safe. Corners mean edges. But the room spun too much. I couldn't see the corner.

So, I crouched by the cupboard.

Hands over head. Knees tight. Counting.

One siren.

Two siren.

Three.

The floor vibrated with the stamp of footsteps fading. The cupboard smelled of polish and dust. My breath rattled.

Then - silence.

The alarm stopped.

The people stopped.

Everything stopped.

And I didn't move.

Not until the world moved first.

◆ ◆ ◆

Maggie's Take - *Don't You Dare Label Him*

The call came at 10:34 a.m.

"There was a fire drill," the teacher said. Her voice was clipped, polite. "Joe didn't cope well."

I took a deep breath. "What does *didn't cope* mean?"

"He wouldn't leave. We had to move the other children. He was hiding. He screamed."

I gripped the phone tighter. "Did anyone warn him first?"

Silence.

Then: "No, it was a surprise. Realism is important."

Realism. Important. I bit down hard on my tongue.

I drove up there.

They met me at the gate. Clipboards held like shields. Sympathetic faces arranged carefully, like masks.

"We think Joe might benefit from a more specialist setting."

I stopped walking. The gravel crunched under my shoes.

"No," I said. "He doesn't need moving. He needs understanding."

They shifted. Looked at each other. Shoes scuffed, pens clicked.
"He's high needs."
"He's high in needs for preparation," I said. "That's different."
They looked at me like I was difficult.
I looked back like I was just getting started.

◆ ◆ ◆

At Home

He was in his blanket tent when I got back. The whale blanket draped over chairs, a little cave in the corner of the room.
I didn't say anything.
I just climbed inside. Cross-legged. Quiet.
The fabric pressed down, muffling the world. Inside smelled like him - cotton, crayons, faint toast crumbs.
We didn't talk.
We didn't need to.
We just breathed.
And the world got a little quieter.

◆ ◆ ◆

Maggie's Notes

•   Fire drill = explosion of senses. Light + sound + touch overload.

•   No warning = no anchor. Always prep.

•   Freeze ≠ defiance. Freeze = stuck.

•   Corners = safety. Provide them.

•   Aftermath: quiet presence > questions.

•   School push = ignorance. Keep fighting.

◆ ◆ ◆

Between Us

Joe's World
A fire drill isn't practice. It's panic. Sirens, flashing lights, smells, touches, voices - all crashing at once. His crouch by the cupboard wasn't misbehaviour. It was survival. Safety isn't just physical. It's sensory, predictable, emotional.

Maggie's World
Maggie hears what the school doesn't: Joe's needs aren't too big - the environment is too unprepared. She refuses the easy answer of "move him." She knows inclusion isn't about location. It's about understanding. And when the world overwhelms him, she doesn't demand words. She sits in his silence.

The Narrators Take

There are few sounds more jarring than a fire alarm.
To Joe, it doesn't just scream. It shatters.
In one second, the world he was managing - just barely - collapses.
The alarm isn't just loud.
It's chaos in coded bursts:
☐ Too bright.
☐ Too sharp.
☐ Too fast.
☐ Too unexpected.
Predictability is Joe's anchor.
When it's cut, he doesn't fall - he freefalls.
He doesn't hear the words "drill."
Doesn't understand the safe faces trying to guide him.
All he knows is escape, but the door feels too far, the corridor too wide, the stares too many.
This isn't just about noise.
It's about control being stolen from him in an instant.

About fear that comes without language.
Maggie isn't there.
And that changes everything.
Because in her absence, all the weight of making sense of it himself presses down.
By the time they explain it's just practice -
the damage is done.

CHAPTER 16: THE BEDTIME BOOK

The Narrators Take
Developmental Note: Regulation Through Ritual – Co-Regulation and Emotional Bonding in Evening Routines

◆ ◆ ◆

Joe's Take - *Same Page, Same Place*

I don't sleep like other people.
Other people close their eyes, and then it's morning. Easy.
I close mine, and then it's everything.
Every sound - the radiator ticking, the fridge humming downstairs, the dog shifting in its basket.
Every shadow - the lamppost outside painting stripes on the wall, the quilt folds looking like mountains.
Every question I didn't ask in the day.
Every rule I broke.
Every rule someone else broke and got away with.
My brain doesn't want the day to end. It wants to replay it. Rewind, pause, check.
Mum used to read with a whisper voice. She said whispering made the stories stretch longer, like chewing gum. The words pulled and pulled, never snapping.
Maggie's voice is louder. Not shouting. But it sits different. It fills the room instead of floating.
Tonight, she's brought a book about a squirrel.

I don't like squirrels. They don't blink right. Their tails twitch like broken signals.

I say, "Pick another."

She tries a bear. A rhyming one.

Rhymes are okay. But only if the rhythm is even.

She misses a beat on page three. My stomach tightens. I pull the quilt to my ears. The fabric smells of washing powder - too strong, not Mum's kind.

She notices. She says, "Want me to start again?"

I nod under the quilt. My breath bounces back warm against my face.

She starts again. Slower. Careful. She finds the pattern.

Page five. She uses the wrong voice for the bear. Too rough. Bears aren't always growly. Some are soft.

I sit up. "No. That's not his voice. He's softer."

Maggie doesn't argue. She changes it. Makes the bear softer. Sleepier. A bit like Dad's voice when he read late and his words slurred with yawns.

I lie back down. My chest stops buzzing.

We finish the book.

I don't say thank you. I don't need to.

She kisses my forehead. Tucks the quilt like Mum used to. Two folds, both sides. The folds pin me safe.

I hum a little. Just a tiny one. My sign that I'm okay.

She hums back.

That's how we end the day now.

Like music, not silence.

◆ ◆ ◆

Maggie's Take - *Words That Work*

Bedtimes are where I feel most lost.

He won't be soothed with the usual things. No warm milk. No counting sheep. No whispered "sweet dreams."

He needs precision. Timing. Voices. Stories that go in a line - not loops.

I picked the squirrel book because I thought it was gentle. But he shot it down with one look. Fair enough.

We tried a bear book. I thought the rhymes would help, keep a rhythm going. But I slipped. Missed a beat. He folded under the covers like I'd dropped a stone into water.

I offered to start again. He let me. That was trust.

So, I slowed down. Felt the rhythm. Matched it to my breathing.

Then I used the wrong voice. I made the bear too rough. He sat up. Corrected me. His voice small but certain: "He's softer."

So, I made the bear softer. Sleepier. A bear that carried warmth instead of growls.

It worked.

When the story ended, he stayed put. No leaving bed. No pacing. No flapping.

I tucked the quilt like I remembered his mum doing. Two folds, one each side. He hummed.

I hummed back.

It wasn't a song anyone else would hear. But it was ours. A kind of duet only we knew.

The first bedtime that didn't end in frustration or flinches. Just hums.

◆ ◆ ◆

Maggie's Notes

- Whisper voice = floats. Louder voice = fills. Adapt tone.

- Wrong rhythm = shutdown. Restart don't rush.

- Characters need the right voices. Soft > rough if he says so.

- Quilt folds = anchor. Replicate exactly.

- Humming = signal of safety. Hum back.

◆ ◆ ◆

Between Us

Joe's World
Night isn't peace. It's replay. Every sound, shadow, and rule breaks sleep into pieces. Books aren't entertainment. They're scaffolding. They only work when the rhythm is steady, and the voices ring true. The quilt folds and the hums are as much part of the story as the words.

Maggie's World
Maggie learns that soothing isn't about guessing. It's about listening, precision, and humility. She doesn't see correction as rejection. She adjusts. When she hums back, she stops being the intruder and becomes part of Joe's ritual.

The Narrators Take

Evening is when the world starts to dim - but for some, the internal noise turns up.
For Joe, bedtime isn't the end of the day.
It's a transition - and transitions are the hardest part.
They mean change.
They mean letting go of the known, even just for the night.
And sometimes they mean thoughts creeping in, ones that didn't have room earlier.
Books aren't just stories.
They're bridges.
Between Maggie and Joe.
Between his racing mind and the world slowing down.
Between the things he feels and the things he can't quite say.
Maggie doesn't always pick the right voice, the right page, the right rhythm.
But she tries.
And that trying becomes part of the ritual.

Joe notices.
Maybe not in words, but in closeness.
In leaning in.
In letting the book finish without flinching.
This is not just a wind-down.
It's a trust exercise.
A slow, quiet dance of co-regulation -
where safety isn't shouted, it's whispered.
And tonight, that's enough.

CHAPTER 17:
THE SLIP-UP

The Narrators Take

Developmental Note: Emotional Overflow and the Power of Repair –
Understanding Behaviour as Communication

◆ ◆ ◆

Joe's Take - *It Wasn't Me; It Was Everything*

I didn't mean to hit her.
It wasn't even a hit. Not really. More like a swing.
A panic swing.
The kind my arms do when everything inside bursts out at once.
The toast was cut wrong. Into triangles. Not squares.
I said it. Twice.
Maggie said, "Triangles are just squares with flair."
I didn't laugh. My stomach turned over. Flair isn't safe. Flair is extra. Flair is wrong.
I told her again. She said we didn't have time to redo it.
That's when it happened.
The fizz started in my chest. The hot buzzing fizz that climbs into my head.
I banged the table. The sound cracked the air. My chair wobbled, legs screeching against the floor. The orange juice tipped, glugging out like a slow spill of fire.
Maggie reached for me. Too fast.
I didn't see her hand. I saw noise coming at me.

And my arm went up to block it. Quick. Sharp. Too sharp.

Her glasses fell. Hit the floor with a clack.

Everything stopped.

The fizz froze. My arms heavy, my chest buzzing like a nest of bees. The sound of the glass rolling on the tiles was the only thing moving.

She didn't shout. She didn't move. Just picked up her glasses and sat down.

I stood still, feeling the whole morning buzz around my ears. Angry bees circling, wings flicking.

Then she said the thing that made the bees quieter.

"Are you safe now, love?"

Her voice was low. Not sharp. Not splintery. Low enough for the bees to settle.

I nodded. Slow. My arm still heavy.

She poured more juice. From the good carton. The one that tastes smooth, not fizzy.

Then, slowly, she cut the toast into squares.

We didn't speak.

But she sat beside me. Not across. Close, but not touching.

I think that meant she wasn't afraid.

◆ ◆ ◆

Maggie's Take -*Stay Soft, Stay Present*

It happened so fast.

One second, we were talking about toast. The next, my specs were halfway across the floor.

He didn't mean to. I could see it in his face the moment it happened - like he'd been taken over by something bigger than him. Shock, not spite.

My first instinct was to raise my voice. To say *That hurt! That's not okay!*

But I stopped myself.

His whole body was coiled like a spring. Arms stiff, eyes wide,

breath ragged. The look wasn't rage. It was fear.
Fear of me. Fear of the world. Fear of himself.
So, I didn't shout. I just sat. Slowly. Let my own heartbeat settle before I spoke.
I gave him a moment to catch up with his own actions.
Then I asked, "Are you safe now, love?"
He nodded. And I believed him.
So, I made more toast. The way he likes it. Squares, not triangles.
Not as a reward. Not because he'd lashed out.
But because I'd missed something.
He wasn't being difficult. He was already overloaded. The wrong shape was just the final straw.
We didn't need a punishment. We needed a pause.
So, I sat beside him. Let my breathing slow. Let his, too.
And we ate toast in quiet. Side by side.

◆ ◆ ◆

Maggie's Notes

- Wrong toast shape = trigger. Details matter.

- "Flair" = unsafe. Avoid jokes about rules.

- Early fizz signs: chest buzzing, banging table, chair wobble.

- Block = fear, not attack.

- Calm tone = de-escalation. Shouting = fuel.

- Sitting beside = trust signal.

◆ ◆ ◆

Between Us

Joe's World

When panic takes over, the body reacts before the mind can catch up. His arm wasn't an attack. It was a shield against what his brain saw as danger. The toast, the juice, the sudden hand - all stacked until his body burst first.

Maggie's World

Maggie wanted to snap back. But she chose calm instead. She saw the difference between violence and overwhelm. By asking about safety, not punishment, she pulled Joe back into control. Sitting beside him turned shame into recovery.

The Narrators Take

There are moments where the lid lifts.
Not because a child wants to "act out,"
but because the world's rules - the sensory ones, the emotional ones - suddenly tip over.
Joe didn't plan to lash out.
There was no strategy.
There was no villain in this moment.
There was a slip-up - maybe a touch too quick, a word too loud, a thing that broke the just-right rhythm.
When you've been living on high alert,
even kindness can land like thunder if it catches you off balance.
And that's what happened.
It's easy, in these moments, to see the behaviour and miss the communication underneath.
Maggie didn't.
She paused.
Even in the hurt, even in the sting,
she saw the boy, not the blow.
Because love - especially trauma-informed love - doesn't just show up when things are tidy.
It shows up in mess. In rupture. In recovery.
And later, when breath steadied and hearts realigned, Joe didn't say "I'm sorry."

He didn't need to.
Because what followed was connection re-threaded -
through shared space, soft eyes, a card without the word "sorry"
but with all the meaning tucked inside.
This is what regulation looks like after rupture:
Not punishment.
But presence.

CHAPTER 18: THE APOLOGY CARD

The Narrators Take

Developmental Note: Emerging Emotional Literacy – Expressing Repair Through Symbolic Gesture

◆ ◆ ◆

Joe's Take - *Not Sorry, But Something Like It*

I didn't sleep well.
Not because I was still angry.
Because I wasn't.
But I'd *done a wrong*.
I'd thrown the book.
I'd shouted.
I'd flapped so hard I hit Maggie's arm.
She didn't shout back.
She just rubbed her arm and sat on the floor near the hallway.
She let me breathe.
I didn't say sorry.
I never say sorry.
It's not a word that works in my mouth.
But today I wanted to make something.
I found my pen tin.
I found my blue card.
I cut a small white square - carefully, evenly.
I drew a football.

One half was red - with a cross through it.
One half was blue - with a heart above it.
I drew a spoon.
I drew a seat by a goal.
And I drew a small stick person with yellow hair. That was her.
Inside, I wrote:
"Only the best managers learn as they go."
I left it on the kitchen table.
Then I walked out the room.

◆ ◆ ◆

Maggie's Take - *He Knew I Needed That*

He hadn't spoken much since the day before.
The "slip."
He didn't mean to hit me - I know that. It was part of the moment.
His fear. His reaction.
But it hurt.
Not just my arm - my heart too.
Because I know he *felt* it.
I didn't want to push him.
I didn't want a sorry forced out of him.
That would be about *me* feeling better. Not him.
So, I gave him space.
And then I saw the card.
Blue, folded neatly.
On the front - a football, a spoon, a little seat.
And a tiny drawing of me.
Inside, it said:
"Only the best managers learn as they go."
I laughed. Properly. Loudly.
Then I cried.
But the good kind.
He didn't need to say sorry.
He already had.

◆ ◆ ◆

Between Us

Joe's Experience
Joe *felt* the mistake - and needed a way to express regret that made sense to him. Words aren't always his tool, but pictures and symbols are his language.

Maggie's Experience
Maggie trusted the space between them. She didn't force a repair - and because of that, Joe came to it in his own way.

The Narrators Take

Children don't always say what they feel.
Not in sentences.
Not in apologies.
Not in ways adults are trained to expect.
But sometimes… they draw it.
In symbols they understand.
In colours that mean something only to them.
In details repeated just-so, because just-so means "I care."
Joe didn't write "Sorry."
He drew Maggie in blue and him in green - her favourite and his safe.
He added a football, because that's where he finds calm.
He added a sun in the top corner, even though it was raining - because she is light, even after storms.
Apology isn't always verbal.
For neurodivergent children, it's often visual. Sensory. Symbolic.
This was Joe's way.
His way of saying, "I know what happened. I wish it hadn't. I still want you near."
And Maggie?
She read every line like a letter.

Because atonement is what happens when the adult doesn't need the word "sorry" to feel the emotion behind it.

This was emotional literacy, developing quietly.

No fanfare. No speech.

Just a card left on a table.

And a relationship quietly strengthened by repair.

CHAPTER 19:
THE VISIT

The Narrators Take

Developmental Note: Navigating Perceived Threats and Fear of Displacement

◆ ◆ ◆

Maggie's Take - *Family Is More Than Just Blood*

The doorbell rang.

I flinched. Not just at the sound - at the *timing*. I knew they were coming, but the bell made it feel too sudden. Too sharp. Like someone had snapped a rubber band right next to my ear.

Joe jumped. His head ducked, hands clamped to his ears, shoulders high and tight like a wave about to break.

I mouthed, *sorry*, before he even looked at me.

When I opened the door, Janine and Raj stood outside. Smart clothes. Kind smiles. Clipboards in hand. They meant well, but they *looked like change.*

I showed them into the lounge. Joe hovered on the stairs, eyes darting between me and the folders under their arms. His knuckles whitened around the banister.

"Let's have a little catch-up," Janine said.

Raj added, "Just to see how things are going. No pressure."

They always said that - *no pressure* - but I felt it anyway.

I perched on the edge of the armchair, the cushion too firm, my hands folded so tight in my lap I could feel my nails pressing half-moons into my skin.

"I'm not his mum," I blurted.

They glanced at each other.

"I know I'm his nan. But I feel like… like I'm messing it all up. The cups, the lights, the cereal box. He flinches, he hides, and I wonder if it's me making it worse."

Raj nodded slowly. "It's not about getting everything perfect. It's about staying in the ring. Showing up, even when you're unsure."

I swallowed hard. My throat ached. "He flinched at the bell. That's on me. I should've prepped him better. I should know by now."

"It's not about fault," Janine said gently. "It's about learning. You're doing great. You care. You adapt. That's what matters."

I wanted to believe her. But my eyes drifted to the wallpaper. There's a tiny rip near the skirting board. Joe spotted it weeks ago, circled it with his finger like it mattered. I still hadn't fixed it.

"He's not a checklist," I muttered.

Raj smiled. "Exactly. And you're not being assessed. You're being supported."

I breathed out. Not full relief. But enough to keep breathing.

◆ ◆ ◆

Joe's Take - *Clipboards Mean Goodbye*

I stayed on the stairs.

They had clipboards.

Clipboards mean change.

At school, when the lady with the clipboard came, I had to move to a different classroom. New smells. New chairs. New lights that buzzed louder.

But the worst was at home.

The night Mum and Dad didn't come back. The police stood in the hall. Their boots were wet. One of them smelled like rain and mud. And the woman with the clipboard - the social worker - wrote things down while I sat on the sofa with my coat still on. She didn't look at me much. Just her papers.

Then she said I had to come with her.

I didn't want to. My chest buzzed, my legs went heavy, but they walked me to her car anyway. Everything smelled like coffee and paper.

Mum and Dad never came back.

After that, clipboards didn't mean notes. They meant endings.

Now they were here. In Maggie's house. And she was talking low, saying she wasn't good enough.

My legs prickled. My chest fizzed like bees again.

So, I went upstairs.

And I packed.

Not folded. Just scooped.

T-shirt. Socks. Blue towel. Visor. Favourite spoon. The bear with one eye.

The bag was heavy. I zipped it anyway. The sound tore the air.

I sat on the top step. The strap dug into my leg. I pressed the bag close. Waited.

When the voices downstairs stopped, I stood. Came down two steps at a time.

"I'm ready," I said.

They all turned.

"Ready for what?" Maggie asked.

"For going. To the new place."

Her mouth opened, then shut.

"No one's going anywhere, love."

"The clipboards," I said. "They're here for moving. That's what happens."

Raj crouched. His knees clicked. "We're not here to move you, Joe. We're here to help Maggie. That's all."

"But people leave when they come. It happened before."

Janine's eyes softened. "That must've been really scary. But we promise - we're not taking you anywhere."

I looked at Maggie.

She looked tired. But strong. Like an old tree that still stands after storms.

"Just me and you," she said. "That's not changing."

The fizz in my chest eased.
I unzipped the bag. Slowly. Let the bear peek out first.

❖ ❖ ❖

Maggie's Notes

- Doorbell = sudden. Warn Joe first.

- Clipboards = danger. Trauma memory from Mum and Dad.

- Packing = survival response, not defiance.

- Reassurance must be plain, concrete.

- Support = not judgment. Remember that for myself too.

❖ ❖ ❖

Between Us

Maggie's World

Maggie's self-doubt is heavy. Every mistake feels like proof she's failing. The professionals remind her that love isn't perfection - it's showing up and adapting. She learns she isn't being graded, she's being supported.

Joe's World

To Joe, clipboards aren't stationery. They're symbols. When his parents died, the social worker and police came with clipboards and took him away. That memory stuck. Packing wasn't drama - it was survival. This time, when adults explained the rules, the pattern cracked. Just enough to unzip the bag.

The Narrators Take

Transitions can bring safety. They can also trigger survival.
For a child who has lost everything once, a knock at the door can

echo like thunder. Even when the visitors smile, even when their words are kind, the clipboard becomes a symbol - not of help, but of loss. Of being moved, again.

In this chapter, Joe meets professionals whose presence resurfaces past trauma: school moves, foster placements, the day everything changed. And Maggie, despite all she's learned, finds herself questioning her own capacity, worried that love and routine might not be enough to meet professional expectations.

Joe's body tells the story: retreating upstairs, packing a bag, assuming the worst. This is not defiance - it's self-preservation. When your story has been one of being uprooted, your nervous system keeps the engine running, always ready to go. Even when you don't want to.

Maggie's side shows something different - but no less vital. It is the rawness of honesty. Her admission that she's not sure if she's good enough isn't weakness. It's the foundation of authentic care. And the social workers - flawed, delayed, but human - finally offer more than checklists: they offer Maggie space to be seen and heard. And to feel enough.

Joe hears none of that. But when the clipboards leave and Maggie doesn't walk away, something quiet shifts.

She stayed.

And for Joe, that is everything.

CHAPTER 20: A VISIT TO THE GRAVE

The Narrators Take

Developmental Note: Meaning-Making Through Ritual – Sensory Grounding and Identity Validation in Bereavement

◆ ◆ ◆

Joe's World

The ground crunched. Not like crisps. Not like cereal. Like old leaves and tiny rocks under my shoes.

Maggie said it was a nice day, but the sky wasn't blue. It was grey, like the bits between channels on an old TV. Still. Heavy.

We parked far away. I counted steps from the car to the gate. Eighty-six. Then the path changed. Stone tiles. Wet edges.

There were rows. Stone after stone. Like books but without spines. I didn't want to look. But I did.

Some had toys. Bears. Plastic flowers. Windmills that didn't turn. Maggie didn't say much. Just pointed to one spot.

I saw the names. His first. Then hers. Then the same last name as mine.

The letters were carved. Neat. But cold.

The grass was short. Too short. And there was a line of ants near the edge. I watched them for a while.

Maggie knelt down. She touched the stone. I didn't.

I stood still.

I could hear a bee. A bird. The wind in the trees. But it all sounded far away, like through a tunnel.

She said, "Do you want to say anything, love?"

I shook my head.

But I wanted to know if they could hear me. Not words. Just sounds. Feelings.

I sat on the bench nearby. It was metal. Cold through my trousers. I didn't like that.

Maggie sat next to me. She didn't try to talk. That was good.

I looked at the clouds. I imagined kicking a ball and it going so high it touched them. I imagined Mum catching it and laughing. I imagined Dad shouting, "That's my boy!" from the other side.

I didn't cry. But my eyes felt thick.

We stayed a while. Until the bench didn't feel as cold.

On the way back, I picked a small white stone and put it in my pocket.

Just to have something.

◆ ◆ ◆

Maggie's World

He didn't ask where we were going. He just got in the car, zipped up his coat, and said, "Route or detour?"

I said route. He nodded. That meant safe.

I'd been putting it off. For him. For me. Mostly me.

I wasn't sure if he understood what the grave meant. But who am I to say what understanding looks like?

He counted steps from the car. Tapped his fingers. Breathed like he was checking something inside him was still working.

When we got there, he stared. His eyes didn't blink much.

I talked to the stone a bit. Nothing fancy. Just updates. Told them Joe was doing okay. Said he eats toast differently. That he watches old football clips on repeat. That he still hates red.

He didn't come close, but he didn't leave either.

When I sat beside him on the bench, I felt something shift.

Not in him. In me.

I'd worried so long about doing everything right. Saying the right things. Filling the silence.

But his silence wasn't empty. It was full of *presence*.

I watched him pick up a stone. He didn't show it to me. Didn't speak.

Just held it in his fist.

And I thought: *That's his goodbye. Or maybe his hello.*

Either way, it was enough.

◆ ◆ ◆

Between *Us*

Joe's Experience

Joe processes grief through senses, not sentences. For him, sound, texture, and stillness say more than words can. Visiting the grave didn't bring a dramatic breakthrough - but it gave space for something unspoken to shift.

Maggie's Experience

Maggie realised that being present was more powerful than saying the perfect thing. Her quiet sitting beside Joe meant more than any speech. She allowed his emotions to unfold in their own time.

The Narrators Take

Grief for a neurodivergent child isn't always expressed the way adults expect.

There's no rulebook for mourning when the world itself often feels too loud, too bright, or too confusing.

Joe didn't need the date.

He didn't need a funeral.

He needed time. Familiarity. Something to touch. Something to carry.

He needed a place to put the feelings he couldn't name.

That's what this visit was.

Not closure - but containment.

A place for questions without answers.

The smells of the cemetery were still and earthy.

A sharp wind carried dampness and something like rust.

The birds weren't singing - they were watching.

Joe noticed that.

He also noticed how Maggie's coat made a different sound when she moved slower.

How her breathing didn't match her words.

How her hand, when it reached for his, felt heavier than usual.

Graves are meant for memory.

But today, they gave Joe a version of now.

A space where the missing people had been,

and in some strange way, still were.

Etched into stone. Written in moss. Trapped in scent.

When Joe placed the stone - blue and smooth and chosen months ago -

it wasn't an offering.

It was a message.

It said:

"I'm still here."

And "I remember."

And maybe, "You mattered."

For Maggie, the visit said something else.

That she was now the keeper of this boy's grief.

The one who would hold both his joy and his silence.

Even on days like this - especially on days like this.

Because sometimes, being steady is the closest thing to being whole.

CHAPTER 21: THE MATCHDAY

The Narrators Take
Developmental Note: Community Reconnection – Exposure to Legacy
Environments with Supportive Peer Recognition

◆ ◆ ◆

Joe's Take - *The Smells, The Steps, The Chants*

There's a smell that lives outside the stadium.
It's hot dogs dripping fat. Cigarette smoke curling sharp in the air.
Bitter steam from burger vans that makes your eyes sting.
I smell it first. Then I hear it.
Rattling badges on boards. Chants bouncing off brick. The thump-thump-thump of feet drumming rhythm on the concrete.
Dad used to walk with that rhythm. Long strides, boots squeaking when the ground was wet. Sometimes I still wait to hear it.
It's too much. It's perfect. It's missing him.
I press the side of my headphones. They don't block it out - just turn it down a notch.
Maggie holds my hand. Not tight. Just enough. Dad never held my hand. He held my shoulder. Firm, steering me through the crowds without words.
Near the wall, a man calls, "Alright, Joe lad!"
That's Deano. He always knew Dad. He talks like he's still talking to him sometimes.
I nod.

He grins, points at Maggie. "That your new signing, eh? Straight in the starting eleven?"

I don't answer. I just hold the scarf closer under my chin. It was Dad's scarf. The wool scratches, the smell's fading, but it still feels like him.

Inside, the turnstiles clank. Metal on metal. Dad always made a joke then: *"Don't get stuck, lad, or we'll have to call the fire brigade."* He's not here to say it.

We find our seats. Same ones Dad brought me to. The girl waves. I wave back once.

Deano leans over with a joke about the away kit looking like custard.

I don't laugh. But I look at him.

Because I know he's trying.

Trying the way Dad used to.

And that counts.

◆ ◆ ◆

Maggie's Take - *They Knew His Dad, and Now, Me*

Deano spotted Joe instantly. So did Graham and Sheila.

They knew his dad. You could see it in their faces - pride, ache, memory all rolled into one. Their eyes softened when they saw him, like they were looking at Joe and his dad at the same time.

But they didn't know me.

I pulled Joe into the row, settled him. He rubbed the edge of the seat with his fingertips, tracing every groove like it mattered.

"Sound bringing him, Mag," Deano said. "The lad needs his footie. His da' would be made up, you know."

My throat caught. I forced a smile.

Sheila leaned in during the warm-up. "You're doing grand, love. It's a lot. But we see you."

Those words hit like warm hands on a cold back.

I wanted to cry. Not out of sadness - out of relief. Someone saw me. Not just Joe's stand-in fumbling through routines. Me.

Graham gave me a nod. Just a nod. But steady. Solid. Like a brick holding up a wall.

As the teams jogged out, floodlights humming, the crowd roared. Joe didn't speak. His eyes tracked the players; his hands rubbed the seat edge in rhythm. He looked calm.

That was more than I could've asked for.

Deano muttered another joke about the ref's haircut. Joe didn't laugh, but he didn't flinch either.

At half-time, when the crowd thinned and the noise dipped, Sheila touched my arm. "How are you really holding up, pet?"

I hesitated. Then whispered, "I feel like I'm messing up half the time. I don't know all his rules. I'm always one step late. And I'm terrified I'm getting it wrong."

Sheila shook her head. "You're here. That's half the battle. Plenty talk the talk. You're walking it."

"I don't feel like I'm enough."

"You're more than enough. He don't need perfect. He needs steady. And you're steady, love. Don't forget that."

I blinked hard, staring at the pitch lights so my eyes didn't spill.

We sat back down. Joe hummed under his breath, scarf clutched close.

For the first time, I didn't just feel like I'd brought him to the game. I felt like we belonged here.

◆ ◆ ◆

Maggie's Notes

- Matchday = storm of smells (hot dogs, smoke, grease, diesel, sugar) + sounds (chants, stomps, clanks).

- Headphones = volume control, not silence.

- Dad's absence = everywhere: scarf, turnstiles, stride, jokes.

- Handhold = anchor.

- Community nods/jokes matter. Joe notices even if he doesn't laugh.

- Sheila's words = lifeline. Steady > perfect.

◆ ◆ ◆

Between Us

Joe's World
Matchday is a sensory storm: smells, chants, scarf scratch, clanking turnstiles. Comforting and overwhelming all at once. But it's also where Dad's absence feels loudest. Every joke, every step, every smell carries his echo. Joe doesn't laugh or join in, but he notices every gesture that tries to fill the gap.

Maggie's World
For Maggie, matchday wasn't just football. It was her first real welcome into Joe's wider world - his dad's mates, his community. Nods, jokes, kind words: tiny things that
anchored her as much as Joe. Sheila reminded her she doesn't need to be perfect. She just needs to be steady. And steady, she can be.

The Narrators Take

Rituals don't always end when the person at the centre of them is gone.
Sometimes they shift. Sometimes they echo.
Sometimes they live on in the people left behind - not perfectly, but faithfully.
For Joe, this wasn't a matchday.
It was the matchday.
A test of whether life could still hold the same shape without the person who carved its outline.
The smells were the same - scorched onions, fried batter, and damp scarves.

The sounds were nearly right - chants carried on scaffolding, ticket stubs ripping like old pages turned too fast.

But something was off.

Something was missing.

Dad.

And yet…

There were people here who remembered.

Faces with the same folds of grief around their smiles.

Voices that greeted Joe like he'd never been gone - like he still belonged.

And through that, so did Maggie. Quietly, uncertainly - but surely.

Maggie wasn't trying to be Dad.

She couldn't be.

But she could listen.

She could learn the rhythm.

She could step into the seat beside Joe and be exactly who he needed her to be -

even if it looked different than before.

Matchday wasn't just a test.

It was a thread.

Stretched thin, maybe, but strong enough to carry memory, connection, and the soft beginnings of something new.

Sometimes progress doesn't cheer.

It just nods, like Deano from two rows down.

It shows up, even when it doesn't know all the chants yet.

And sometimes, that's more than enough.

CHAPTER 22: ONE MATCH AT A TIME

The Narrators Take

Developmental Note: Emotional Insight – Internalisation and Symbolic Expression of Transition and Acceptance

◆ ◆ ◆

Joe's Take - *New Player, Same Shirt*

The house is quiet.

No shouting fans. No lights flashing. No smells of chips or pies or salt.

Just me and Maggie. And the echo of the day.

I take off my coat one button at a time.

I put my shoes next to each other, toes facing the door. That's how I like it.

Maggie switches on the side lamp. Not the big one. That's good.

The room glows orange like warm toast.

We don't talk.

We don't need to.

She goes into the kitchen and makes two hot chocolates. Mine has one big marshmallow in the middle. That's how I like it too.

I sit on the beanbag.

My ears are still buzzing from the crowd. The claps. The goal song.

The man behind us shouting too loud about offsides.

And Deano's joke.

He said:

"Why don't skeletons go to the match?"
Then laughed before he finished:
"Cause they ain't got the guts!"
I didn't laugh. But I remembered it. And that counts.
I still hear the siren from the street. It makes me clench.
Every time.
But Maggie does the thing.
She presses her hand softly against mine. Doesn't talk. Just stays.
The siren fades.
My breath evens out.
And then I say it.
The thing I've been thinking for weeks.
"You know when your best player leaves the club?" I ask.
Maggie looks at me, waiting.
"And you don't want them to go. But they do. And it hurts. And then the team signs someone new and it's weird. 'Cause they're not the old one. But you still go the match. And you still cheer. Even when it feels different."
She nods.
"It's like that."
She doesn't speak.
So, I keep going.
"You're the new player. But you're getting better every week."
She wipes her glasses.
I pretend not to see.
Then she says, "I'll always be your number 2."
I blink.
"Why not number 1?"
She grins.
"Number 1's already taken. Forever. I just want to be good enough to play beside him. In your squad."
And I say, quietly but certain,
"You are, Nan."

◆ ◆ ◆

Maggie's Take - *That Was His I Love You*

He didn't say *I love you.*
He doesn't say that.
But that was it.
That was his version.
His way.
His language.
And it landed. Right in my chest.
All the questions I've had - Am I doing this right? Will he ever trust me? Can I really fill these shoes?
They don't matter anymore. Not tonight.
Because I heard him.
Because he sees me.
Tomorrow will come, and we'll face it together - not perfect, not easy - but together.
One match at a time.
And as I rinsed the mugs later, I realised something else.
It wasn't the football metaphor that undid me.
It wasn't even the hot chocolate with the marshmallow.
It was the word.
Nan.
The first time he's ever called me that.
And I don't think I'll ever need anything sweeter.

◆ ◆ ◆

The Narrators Take

Closure is rarely a final act.
It's not a door slamming shut or a speech that fixes everything.
It's quieter than that.
It happens in layers-with socks pulled up in silence, with dinner eaten without prompting, with stories shared when no one asked.
Tonight, Joe found words.
Not just any words-his words.

Football words. Transfer window metaphors. Squad changes.
Not a single mention of grief, but every sentence soaked in it.
For Maggie, the match was another step. But the real shift came after.
At home.
When the lights were low and Joe flinched at the siren-still-but Maggie no longer froze.
She responded right.
Because she'd learned, moment by moment, what "right" meant for Joe.
This wasn't the end of a journey.
It was a checkpoint.
A chance to look back and realise that between the routines, the missteps, the wrong cups and the worn-out lists…
something had changed.
Joe had let her in.
And in Joe's world, that's not done with hugs or confessions.
It's done through language that feels safe.
Through metaphor and structure and stories that mean more than they say.
And Maggie-exhausted, unsure, never claiming to be perfect-heard it.
Not just the words, but what they held.
"You are, Nan."
No big finale.
Just four syllables soaked in a season's worth of trying.
And the warm, quiet truth that the new doesn't erase the old-it honours it, and then gently carries forward…
One match at a time…. One Moment at a Time.

❖ ❖ ❖

A Note from Joe

When I came here, I didn't know if it was safe.

Everything smelled different. The kettle sounded wrong. The toast was cut the wrong way. I thought the clipboards meant I'd have to leave again.

I called her *Maggie.* Because she wasn't Mum. And she wasn't Nan. She was new. New is danger.

Now it's different.

She knows about the blue cup. She lets me write the lists. She sits with me when the noises get too big. She doesn't laugh when I flap or hum. She waits. She learns.

I called her *Nan.*

The first time, it felt heavy. But right.

What I look forward to:

More matches. More hot chocolate. More lists that we write together.

And knowing that even if things still change, she won't.

◆ ◆ ◆

A Note from Maggie

When Joe came to me, I was scared. I loved him, but I didn't know his rules. I kept getting it wrong - the cups, the lights, the toast, the timing. I thought maybe I was hurting him more than helping.

I called myself *just a stand-in.* Someone filling shoes far too big for me.

Now it's different.

I know that lists are lifelines. That flapping is release. That silence can be louder than words. I've learned that I don't need to be perfect. I just need to be steady.

He called me *Nan.*

The first time, it undid me. Because it meant I was his, after all.

What I look forward to:

Being his anchor, even when the world feels stormy. Sitting beside him at Goodison. Learning new rules every day.

And reminding myself that love doesn't always sound like *I love*

you.
Sometimes it sounds like, *"You are, Nan."*

◆ ◆ ◆

Notes for You

For Children who are Neurodiverse

We see you.
We know that the world can feel loud, bright, and too fast sometimes. We know how much the little things matter - the right cup, the right seat, the right list. That doesn't make you difficult. That makes you *you.*
We see your routines, your bravery, your way of making the world make sense. We understand that flapping, humming, or going flat isn't bad behaviour - it's how you keep yourself safe.
You are not broken. You are not less.
You are noticed, valued, and loved exactly as you are.

For Families living with someone who is Neurodiverse

We see you.
We know it isn't always easy. There are days when you question yourself, when you feel like you're getting it wrong, when you worry if you're enough.
But being steady matters more than being perfect. Showing up matters more than always knowing what to do. Love, patience, and learning one step at a time make the difference.
We see the strength it takes to keep going, the creativity in how you adapt, and the quiet victories that nobody else notices.
You are not failing. You are not alone.
You are part of a team, and your steadiness is everything.

For Teachers, Friends, and the Wider World

We see you.

Maybe Joe's world feels new to you. Maybe you've learned something different about how children think, feel, and cope. What looks small from the outside can be huge inside. What looks like fussiness is often safety.

We see your efforts to listen, to adapt, to welcome difference. Every smile, every pause, every moment of patience helps someone like Joe feel safe.

You are part of the change. You are part of the support.

And you matter more than you realise.

◆ ◆ ◆

Sensory Index: Joe's Journey Through Senses

A chapter-by-chapter summary of sensory experiences that shape Joe's world.

1. The New House

Triggers: unfamiliar smells, doorbell sound, cold walls, echoing rooms
Supports: Nan's warm blanket, familiar rucksack
Responses: caution, hypervigilance, quiet withdrawal

2. The First Breakfast

Triggers: cutlery scraping, wrong cereal box colour, loud spoon clinks
Supports: patterned place mat, routine order
Responses: frustration, internal overwhelm, early masking

3. The Bus Ride
Triggers: engine rumble, chatter, changing smells at each stop
Supports: headphone padding, counting street signs
Responses: coping through focus, zoning out

4. The Shopping List
Triggers: fluorescent lights, shopping trolley squeaks, unpredictable noises
Supports: laminated list, clear expectations
Responses: momentary overload, then structured calm

5. New School Shoes
Triggers: touching feet, fluorescent shop lights, strong smells of polish
Supports: choice between two options, familiar routine with laces
Responses: irritation, avoidance, eventual acceptance

6. The Appointment
Triggers: phone ringing, antiseptic smells, crinkly paper on bed
Supports: Nan's soothing voice, fidget stone
Responses: overstimulation, shutdown behaviour

7. Wrong Cup
Triggers: visual mismatch (wrong colour), texture
Supports: routine reinforcement
Responses: distress, escalation, withdrawal

8. Red Coat Day
Triggers: loud voices at school gate, coat texture, change in uniform order
Supports: scarf routine, teacher's calm tone
Responses: unease, seeking control through routine

9. A New Sound
Triggers: new headphones - too crisp, missing old comforting static
Supports: gradual re-familiarisation
Responses: suspicion, slow trust in new item

10. The List
Triggers: being interrupted, losing track of the list order
Supports: ability to rewrite, visual order
Responses: tension, recovery through recontrol

11. A Day Without Maggie
Triggers: unfamiliar car engine, strange male voice, late timing
Supports: familiar cushion, quiet corner
Responses: panic, regression, flight behaviour

12. Wrong Words
Triggers: Maggie says something different than expected phrase
Supports: calm space, breathing regulation
Responses: confusion, questioning safety

13. The Invitation
Triggers: colourful envelope, party noises imagined
Supports: time to process, visual rehearsal
Responses: conflicted anticipation, reluctance

14. Pancake Tuesday
Triggers: sizzling pan, sweet syrup smell, new textures
Supports: clear turn-taking, option to observe first
Responses: curiosity, step-by-step participation

15. The Fire Drill
Triggers: sudden alarm, crowd movement, teacher shouting
Supports: post-event decompression, headphones (delayed)
Responses: meltdown, silent recovery

16. Bedtime Book
Triggers: book page rustle, light brightness
Supports: predictability, chosen story, scent of pillow
Responses: calm, connection

17. The Slip Up
Triggers: wrong approach during moment of stress
Supports: Maggie's calm de-escalation, no raised voice

Responses: physical lashing out, deep guilt

18. The Apology Card
Triggers: emotional vulnerability, internal pressure
Supports: symbolic expression (football theme), no forced language
Responses: relief, rebuilding connection

19. The Visit
Triggers: knock at door, clipboards, formal voices
Supports: post-visit reassurance, Maggie's presence
Responses: panic, bag-packing, fear of removal

20. A Visit to the Grave
Triggers: wind across skin, silence, memory scent
Supports: Maggie's distance/respect, scarf comfort
Responses: deep sensory memory, emotional shift

21. Matchday Debut
Triggers: hot dog smoke, clanking turnstiles, chanting
Supports: headphones, scarf, crowd rhythm
Responses: nostalgic grief, cautious joy

22. One Match at a Time
Triggers: night quiet, ambulance siren outside
Supports: Maggie's response, shared silence
Responses: verbalisation of love, calm acceptance

◆ ◆ ◆

Glossary of Key Terms

Neurodivergent – A term that describes people whose brains work differently from what is considered "typical." This includes autism, ADHD, dyslexia, and many other conditions.

Neurological – Relating to the brain and nervous system. In this book, it connects to how Joe's brain processes information: sights, sounds, textures, routines, and emotions. His neurological wiring shapes the way he experiences the world.

Neurotypical – A term used to describe people whose brain processes, learning styles, and behaviours fall within what society considers the "typical" range. In contrast to neurodivergence, neurotypical development usually follows predictable patterns that schools and systems are built around.

Sensory Processing – How the brain takes in and organises information from the senses (sight, sound, touch, taste, smell, balance, body awareness). For some people, certain senses can feel too strong or too weak.

Dysregulation – When emotions, thoughts, or body responses feel overwhelming and difficult to manage. This might look like meltdowns, withdrawal, or physical outbursts.

Masking – Hiding or suppressing natural behaviours in order to "fit in." Masking can be exhausting and often leads to burnout.

Self-Regulation – Ways of calming the body and mind after stress. For Joe, this might be flapping hands, counting, or using headphones.

Co-Regulation – When another person (like Maggie) helps provide calm, structure, or reassurance so Joe can feel safe again.

Routine – A predictable sequence of events or actions. Routines help create security and reduce anxiety.

Trigger – Something that sets off an emotional or sensory reaction. For Joe, this might be the wrong cup, loud alarms, or changes to plan.

Safe Item – An object that provides comfort or predictability (like

Joe's scarf, headphones, or favourite seat).

Meltdown – An intense response to overwhelm. Different from a tantrum, meltdowns are not chosen - they are the body's way of coping when it has had too much.

◆ ◆ ◆

Reading Guide

This book is designed to be read in different ways:

With Families

Pause after each chapter and ask: "What did Joe notice? What did Maggie notice? What do we notice?"

Use the sensory index to reflect on your own family's routines and what makes them feel safe.

Talk about differences between neurodivergent and neurotypical ways of experiencing the world. Neither is wrong - they're just different.

In Classrooms or Groups

Read Joe's part aloud and ask children what they imagine he is feeling through his senses.

Discuss Maggie's part to highlight how adults can support without "fixing."

Invite children to share their own experiences: "What helps you when things feel too loud or too much?"

Compare perspectives: How might a neurotypical child and a neurodivergent child see the same moment differently?

For Professionals

Use chapters as case studies for reflective practice.

Focus on the Narrator's Takes as a training lens to link behaviours with regulation needs.

Identify when your systems are built around neurotypical expectations, and consider how to flex for neurodivergent needs.

Celebrate small wins (like three bites at breakfast) as big developmental steps.

◆ ◆ ◆

Closing Message

This is Joe's story.

It is not every story.

Neurodivergence is diverse. Each child, each family, each journey will be different. What matters is not perfection, but presence. Not fixing, but listening.

If you are neurotypical, you may see the world through different rhythms and rules. If you are neurodivergent, you may find pieces of yourself in Joe's journey. Both perspectives matter. Both deserve respect.

If this book does anything, let it be this:

To remind us that children are not problems to solve, but people to understand.

And that love, patience, and steady effort - one moment at a time - can build a bridge between worlds.

◆ ◆ ◆

Conversation Points - Talking About Joe's Story

These questions are not a test. They are for talking, listening, and sharing ideas.

Joe's World

- What helps Joe feel safe when things change?

- Why do little details (like the right cup, toast shape, or list) matter so much to him?

- How does Joe show his feelings without using words?

- What does it mean when Joe goes "flat" or flaps his hands?

Maggie's World

- How did Maggie learn to listen to Joe in *his* way?

- What mistakes did she make? How did she fix them?

- Why do you think Maggie sometimes felt unsure?

- What made Maggie feel part of Joe's community at the match?

Football and Belonging

- Why is football so special for Joe?

- How does football help him remember his dad?

- What did it mean when Maggie said she was "number 2" in Joe's team?

- Why was it so important when Joe called her *Nan* for the first time?

Feelings and Trust

- How is a meltdown different from being "naughty"?

- Why doesn't punishment always help when someone is upset?

- What small things did Maggie do to help Joe calm down?

- What does "going at someone's speed" mean to you?

Your World

- What helps *you* feel calm when your day changes?

- Have you ever felt safe because someone listened to you properly?

- How can you help a friend who finds noise or change difficult?

- What's one thing you will see differently after reading Joe's story?

◆ ◆ ◆

Notes From Our World

Use these pages to write down moments that felt important - or routines, emotions, and breakthroughs in your world. You could jot down:

Something new you learned about your child or student

A moment of connection

A challenge you overcame together

A routine that helped

A breakthrough that surprised you

This is your space to reflect, just as Joe and Maggie do.

Printed in Dunstable, United Kingdom